VANISHED

VANISHED

A NOVEL BY

KATE BRIAN

SIMON & SCHUSTER BFYR

New York   London   Toronto   Sydney

SIMON & SCHUSTER BFYR

An imprint of Simon & Schuster Children's Publishing Division
1230 Avenue of the Americas, New York, New York 10020

For information about special discounts for bulk purchases, please contact
Simon & Schuster Special Sales at 1-866-506-1949 or
business@simonandschuster.com.
The Simon & Schuster Speakers Bureau can bring authors to your live
event. For more information or to book an event, contact the Simon &
Schuster Speakers Bureau at 1-866-248-3049 or visit our website
at www.simonspeakers.com.

Produced by Alloy Entertainment
151 West 26th Street, New York, NY 10001

Typography by Andrea C. Uva
The text of this book was set in Filosofia.
Manufactured in the United States of America
2 4 6 8 10 9 7 5 3 1
Library of Congress Control Number: 2010929992
ISBN 978-1-4169-8471-9
ISBN 978-1-4424-0948-4 (eBook)

For Lanie

VANISHED

SILENCE

I couldn't sustain this for much longer. The rushing thoughts. The shallow breathing. The pounding, pounding, pounding in my brain. It made me light-headed, dizzy, and faint. All night I'd been trapped inside my eight-by-eight single room, watching the digital clock on my desk slowly count the minutes. Waiting. Waiting every moment for the phone to ring, for a text to come in. Waiting for any kind of direction.

I sat on the edge of my bed, still wearing my clothes from the night before, my palms slick with sweat as I clutched my cell phone. The same, stark message had been staring up at me all night long. Now the first pink light of morning crept through my window and still, nothing changed.

WE HAVE NOELLE LANGE. IF YOU GO TO THE POLICE, SHE DIES. IF YOU GO TO HER FAMILY, SHE DIES. IF YOU GO TO THE

HEADMASTER, SHE DIES. YOU WILL FOLLOW OUR EVERY INSTRUCTION TO THE LETTER, OR SHE WILL DIE. THE GAME IS ON, REED BRENNAN. THE PRIZE? NOELLE'S LIFE.

I rose and paced across the tiny expanse of my dorm room. The message was horrifying. And baffling. Who had sent it? Why? Where had they taken Noelle? Why were they doing this to us? What did they want with Noelle? Why would anyone want her dead? I couldn't stop thinking about the night before when my friends and I had stolen up to the Billings Chapel in the woods off campus for a meeting of our secret organization, the Billings Literary Society. Everything had been fine until the wind had taken out some of our candles. That was when the banging had started. Then the screams. In the total darkness, my Billings sisters and I had panicked, fear pulsating off us. What if I had reached for Noelle in the middle of it? Would I have been able to hold on to her? Would she still be here right now?

I shoved my free hand into my dirty brown hair, holding it back from my face. Did this have anything to do with the Billings Literary Society? Had the Billings Alums who didn't approve of our secret society taken Noelle to prove some kind of point? If I'd never started this thing up in the first place, we wouldn't have even been up at the chapel. Noelle would have been here on the Easton Academy campus, huddled away in her single room, studying or listening to music or tweeting about how damn boring Easton is during the winter. Was this my fault? Was this really all my fault?

But no. Someone had left the BLS book for me. Someone wanted me to re-establish the secret society. And Noelle had joined of her own free will. Besides, maybe it had nothing to do with the society. Maybe if we hadn't been in the old Billings Chapel last night they would have taken her from her room or the library or wherever she might have been otherwise. Maybe I wasn't to blame.

Not everything was always my fault. All evidence to the contrary.

But even if, by some slim chance, this wasn't my fault, I was still the one who had to deal with it. I was the one the kidnappers had chosen to contact. Why? Why me? I hugged myself tightly and turned toward the opposite wall. I had to keep moving, even if I had no direction, even if everything I did was pointless. The doubting, the regret, the terror, the endless questions—it all came in waves, crashing down on my chest over and over and over again until I felt as if I couldn't breathe.

But even worse than the hindsight was the current state of total silence. It had been seven hours since the text had come through. Seven hours of nothing. Where were these all-important instructions? If the "game" was, in fact, "on," then it wasn't a very exciting one. The text said that Noelle's life depended on my doing something, but what? When were they going to tell me? What was with the extreme delay?

I let out an angry growl and hurled the phone onto the bed. Even in my frustration I had the restraint not to throw it too hard. It was, after all, my only connection to my best friend. All along the hallways of Pemberly Hall, people were starting to stir. Someone's stereo flipped on, a hair dryer hummed a few doors down, the scent of espresso wafted my way from under my door, thanks to the new coffeemaker Ivy Slade's roommate had received for Christmas. Outside the window, the sky was bright white now, screaming of impending snow. I blinked my dry eyes a few times, the skin around them tight and tired. What was I supposed to do? Get dressed and go about my day? Pretend as if nothing was wrong?

Or stay here and wait?

I turned and looked at the phone.

"Ring," I said firmly under my breath. "Ring. Beep. Vibrate. Do something!"

It stared back at me, silent and dark.

"Screw this."

I jammed open the accordion door on my closet and pulled out the first items of clothing I saw: a pair of dark green cords and a black turtleneck sweater. I was just yanking on the pants when I realized I should probably change my underwear. I shuffled over to my dresser and yanked open my underwear drawer. The red, lace tank top I had bought in New York on a dare from Noelle a few weeks earlier practically sprang out of the overpacked space. Instantly I started to cry.

There was a quick knock at the door and it started to open.

"One second!" I said, springing for it and slamming it closed again.

"Ow. Reed! It's just me!" Ivy said.

"I'm half dressed!" I replied, trying to keep the tears out of my voice. "Hang on."

I wiped my face with the backs of my hands and took a deep breath, rounding my shoulders and looking in the mirror. I was a complete and total wreck. Dark circles framed my bloodshot eyes. My nose was redder than the lacy underwear still clutched in my fist, and my hair was knotted and dirty around my face.

Quickly, I yanked on a pair of cotton underwear, fastened my pants around my waist, and ran a brush through my hair, pulling it back in a tight ponytail. Then I plopped a few drops of Visine in each eye, blinked at the ceiling a few times, and breathed in.

Time to start lying my ass off.

"Hey!" I said with a bright smile, opening the door. "Sorry about that. I was kind of underwear-free."

"No problem." Ivy stepped into the room, her dark eyes trained on my face. "Are you okay?"

She looked perfect, of course, her black hair shining on her shoulders, her ivory skin scrubbed and blushed, mascara accentuating her gorgeous eyes. She wore a black wool skirt, black knee-high boots, and a red sweater. Like today was not only a normal day, but maybe even a special one. She had her white coat slung over one arm and her Stella McCartney bag on her shoulder.

"Yeah. I just got something in my eye," I lied, closing the door behind her. "I was trying to use drops to flush it out, but no luck."

I scrounged an old paper napkin out of the side pocket on my messenger bag and used it to blow my nose.

"Getting stuff in your eyes is the worst."

"Totally," I said.

Yeah right. As opposed to, say, getting kidnapped in the middle of the night right out from under your friends' noses? As opposed to being the person the elusive kidnappers had contacted and then forgotten about? "The worst" was kind of relative at the moment.

Ivy crossed her arms more tightly, holding her coat against her stomach, and walked casually past me into the room. She looked back at me over her shoulder with narrow, almost sly eyes. "So?"

My heart skipped erratically.

"So, what?" I asked, even though I knew exactly what "so" meant.

Her eyebrows arched. "Have you heard from Noelle?"

I turned my back to her and looked in the mirror again, my palms slick with sweat. I fished a lip gloss out of my vinyl cosmetics bag, but my hand was shaking, so I put it down. I had come up with a cover story for this, hadn't I? Sometime around three a.m. when I'd hidden Noelle's bag and phone under a stack of sweaters on the top shelf of my closet?

"Yeah," I said finally. "She came by last night to get her stuff."

"She did?" Ivy said, her tone accusatory. "Why didn't you come tell me?" She walked up behind me, the better to glare at my reflection in the mirror.

"Sorry. It was late," I said with a shrug. "I figured you were asleep. It's not as if you've ever cared that much about Noelle anyway."

Ivy glanced away. She couldn't argue with that. "So what happened?"

"She had to go home for a few days. Some kind of family emergency," I replied, steeling myself long enough to finally apply the lip gloss.

Ivy looked up at me through her long lashes. "What? That makes no sense."

"I don't know what to tell you. That's what she said," I replied, rummaging through my closet for a pair of sneakers. I wondered if she'd noticed that I'd yet to really look her in the eye.

"But then why did she disappear from the chapel? And why did she leave her bag and cell phone there?" Ivy asked, dropping her coat and bag on my bed.

"Oh, that."

"Yeah. That," Ivy said acerbically. Clearly she was annoyed, but I knew her annoyance was directed at Noelle and not at me. Ivy was perpetually irritated with Noelle. Or angry with her. Or full-on furious with her. It just depended on the day and the situation.

"That was a prank," I told her, looking up briefly. "She was trying to make it look like she was grabbed or something, just to mess with us. After all the candles went out, she snuck out the back door and came down to campus to wait for us, but when she got there she got a call from her mom on her backup phone and she had to leave right away."

Ivy's eyes narrowed as she pondered this. My ribs rattled with each pound of my heart. She had to buy the story. She had to. It was the best one I had. The only one.

"Unbelievable," she said finally, shaking her head. "She scared the crap out of us. God. What a total bitch."

"I know! I know," I said, breathing a slight sigh of relief. "I told her how everyone was freaking out. She felt really bad about it."

"I'll bet," Ivy said sarcastically.

Something inside of me snapped. "I know you don't like her, but do you really have to call her names all the time?" I demanded. "She *is* one of my best friends."

Ivy looked stunned for a moment. Not surprising. I wasn't normally big on the outbursts. But Noelle didn't deserve to be called a bitch. Especially not now. Especially when she might already be . . .

I swallowed hard and looked at the floor. Ivy threw up her hands in surrender. "Sorry. I'll try to control myself from now on. But if she keeps pulling crap like this I make no guarantees."

She crossed to my bed, which was still made since I hadn't slept at all last night, and sat down. As she leaned back on her hands she knocked my phone across the bed toward the wall. My heart flew into my throat as she turned to pick it up. The "game on" text was still up on the screen.

"I got it!" I said, lunging at her and snatching the cell away before she could look at it.

"Wow," Ivy said. "Grab much?"

I forced a laugh that sounded more like a strangled cough, and shoved the phone into the depths of my bag.

"Come on," I said, grabbing my coat off the back of my desk chair. "I'm starving."

"Me too. I hope they have French toast this morning," Ivy said, bouncing off my bed. Her total lack of sadness, foreboding, and fear made me feel even more miserable and more alone. "I seriously can't believe Noelle, though," she said as she slipped past me out the door, shrugging one arm into the sleeve of her coat. "Although I guess I shouldn't be surprised. When has she ever given a crap about anyone other than herself? Sooner or later that girl is going to get hers."

So much for controlling herself.

She shoved her other arm into her coat as I banged the door closed behind us, biting down on my tongue to keep from lashing out again or crying, or both. Laying into Ivy was not going to help Noelle. I had to try to stay calm and in control. I had to make sure I was ready for whatever was coming next.

PRIME SUSPECTS

Josh Hollis sat alone at a corner table in the dining hall, his shoulders hunched, his doughnuts untouched. But the moment Ivy and I emerged from the buffet-style food line, his posture straightened. My heart thumped extra hard. He was waiting for me. Waiting for news. Josh was the only person who knew about what had really happened to Noelle. He'd been with me when the text had come in, and from the looks of his rumpled blue sweater and waxy skin, he'd spent the night in much the same way I had: sleeplessly.

"Are you guys going to go to the Valentine's Day dance next weekend?" Ivy asked casually.

I blinked. Dances and chocolates and flowers were about the furthest thing from my mind right then. But now that I looked around the stone-walled room, I saw that a few glittery red and pink hearts dangled from the ceiling here and there. A big white banner had been strung across the back wall, inviting us all to the annual Sweethearts

Dance next Saturday night, and there was a distinctly flirtatious vibe in the air—lots of blushing and giggling and whispering.

"I don't know," I replied, trying not to wonder whether Noelle would even be alive next Saturday night. "I didn't even realize it was February."

Ivy laughed. "You need coffee. Go ahead. He's waiting for you." She nudged me with her elbow, carefully balancing her tray of French toast and fruit. "I'll sit with the girls and tell them what happened with Noelle."

"Thanks," I replied. "Try not to bash her in the process."

She smirked. "I'll try."

Normally, I might have made sure that Ivy was truly okay with me going over and sitting alone with her ex-boyfriend, who was now my current boyfriend. But today, I didn't have it in me to be overly solicitous. I walked over to Josh's table, dropped my tray of Cheerios down across from his tray of doughnuts, and sat.

"Anything?" he asked hopefully, raising his eyebrows.

I shook my head once. "Nope."

His fingers found mine under the table. His green eyes were rimmed with red as he stared into mine. "It's going to be okay," he said. "We're going to figure this out."

My throat squeezed closed and fresh tears stung my eyes. All around me there was laughter and conversation and the clatter of silverware against ceramic plates. Some guy at the next table laughed so hard, apple juice came spurting out his nose. But I barely saw or heard any of it.

"How?" I asked.

"I've been thinking about this all night," Josh said, releasing my hand and sitting back in his chair. "We need to start by making a list of her enemies. And yours."

"My enemies?" I asked, the words crackling over my tongue. "Why mine?"

"Because," Josh said, like it was so obvious, "they may have taken her, but they're torturing you. Whoever did this either hates Noelle, or you, or both of you."

I swallowed hard and sat back in my chair, slumping until the base of my skull rested on the top of the chair back. "Could be a long list."

Josh smirked and reached for his coffee, glancing around surreptitiously. "You should sit up."

"Why?" I snapped unnecessarily. Josh, however, either didn't notice or didn't care.

"Because whoever did this might be watching you right now," he said, hiding his lips behind his coffee cup. "We don't want them to know that I know what's going on. And you also don't want to look all desperate."

An incredible, sweet warmth filled my chest, like someone was baking fresh cinnamon rolls in there. Thank heaven for Josh. At least he was thinking clearly. I pushed my exhausted body up until I was seated on the edge of my chair.

"I don't know what I would do if you hadn't been there when I got that text," I said under my breath. I pushed my spoon into my cereal, making a show of being normal. "I don't think I could do this alone."

"You're never alone," Josh replied firmly. "Not anymore."

"Thanks," I said, my voice thick.

"So?" Josh prompted, taking a sip of his coffee and placing the cup down. He folded his arms on the table and glanced around. "Who are your prime suspects?"

He had a smile on his face for show, and looked for all the world as if he really could be discussing the dance.

"Well, there's the reject table," I said, tilting my head slightly toward the center of the room. Missy Thurber, Constance Talbot, and London Simmons—the three former Billings residents who hadn't made the cut into the Billings Literary Society—all sat at their usual table, and they were all casting deadly glares at me as always. Josh whistled quietly.

"Wow. That last evil stare glanced off you and hit me," he joked, shifting in his seat. "But what do you mean, the reject table? Since when are those guys rejects? I mean, I know Missy isn't your favorite person, but I thought you and Constance were all buddy-buddy, at least."

My heart skipped ten thousand beats. Josh didn't know about the Billings Literary Society. It was, after all, a secret. But almost all my prime suspects, as he called them, were somehow related to the BLS. If he was going to help me find Noelle, he had to know. Not everything, but at least the basics.

I took a deep breath and sat forward. "I kind of started a secret society," I whispered.

"What?!" Josh blurted.

Half the dining hall went silent and turned to stare. Josh's face turned bright red and he leaned forward, so close our foreheads almost touched.

"What?" he hissed quietly.

"It's a long story," I said. "But basically, there are only eleven members, so some of my friends"—I pronounced the last word through my teeth as I cast my glance toward the reject table—"didn't get in."

"Whoa."

Josh picked up a doughnut, and took a big bite. "That's a motive."

"Kind of, yeah," I said, chewing on my bottom lip.

"You *are* going to tell me more about this later," he said, powdered sugar clinging to his lips.

"We'll see," I said hesitantly.

"Okay. Who else?" he asked.

"Well, some of the Billings Alumnae threatened us recently," I said, poking at a few Cheerios with my spoon. "They blame us for Billings House being torn down."

"Which ones?" Josh asked.

"Paige Ryan, Susan Llewellyn, and Demetria Rosewell," I replied.

Another whistle from Josh. "Can't get more connected than that. The Rosewells own half the defense contracts in the country. She could probably order up her own team of Navy SEALs if she wanted. Could you imagine if a team of SEALs grabbed Noelle? She could be in Kuwait by now."

I dropped my spoon. It clanged loudly against the edge of my bowl. "Really not making me feel better here, Josh," I said.

"Sorry. Sorry." He placed what was left of his doughnut down on his plate and raised his hands in surrender. "Anyone else?"

Just then there was a loud, familiar guffaw from the direction of the food line. I turned to look and saw Gage Coolidge yucking it up with Sawyer and Graham Hathaway—two guys who had been my friends until Graham had pummeled Josh for a past offense against his sister, Jen, who passed away last summer. And until I had broken Sawyer's heart by getting back together with Josh. All three of them froze in their tracks and stopped laughing when they saw me and Josh. Then Gage slapped Graham's chest with the back of his hand and led him off in the opposite direction. Sawyer stood there for a moment, looking at me in this sort of forlorn way, before ducking his blond head and trudging after them.

"I guess *he* kind of hates me right now," I said, facing forward again.

"Sawyer?" Josh asked. "You think he's the evil mastermind behind this?"

I gave him a small, sad, smile. "Not really. But I've been fooled before."

Josh and I looked at each other for a long moment, thinking of all the people we'd lost . . . and of all the people we'd trusted who'd turned out to be completely bat-crap crazy.

"Well, if it makes you feel any better, I guess Gage has chosen the Hathaway brothers over me," Josh said.

"Wow. A major loss," I joked flatly.

"It's definitely a blow," Josh replied, a teasing glint in his eye.

We both smiled wanly at our halfhearted attempt at lightness. Then I took a sip of my juice and looked away, feeling guilty for even trying when Noelle was out there somewhere suffering.

"I'd say this Billings Alumnae thing is your best bet," Josh said, wiping his fingers on a napkin. "Those women have money, power, connections, and a crap load of time on their hands. Plus, if they still care about a dorm enough to threaten you, then clearly they've got some serious issues."

"You're right," I said. "One of them just might be crazy enough to do something like this." A slight thrill of excitement edged out some of the dread from my heart. Now we were getting somewhere. If I could go on the offensive, take some control over the situation, maybe I could end this thing before it even really got started. "I'll see what I can find out."

"Just be careful, Reed," Josh said. "These people clearly aren't messing around. I don't think I could take it if you disappeared on me."

"Understood," I said, reaching for his hand and lacing my fingers through his. "But don't worry. I promise I've put my damsel in distress days behind me."

FIRST ASSIGNMENT

This was probably a very bad idea. An extremely very bad idea. But as I trudged through the woods alone that night, my hood drawn over my head, my face bent toward the ground against the swirling snow, I was certain it was also the right thing to do. Paige Ryan knew something. Why else would she have agreed to meet me so easily? Why else would she have even picked up the phone when I'd called? The girl hated my guts for "stealing" Upton Giles away from her and her friends down on St. Barths over Christmas break. She hated me for the fact that her mother had been locked up for trying—repeatedly—to murder me.

Yeah. The girl had a skewed sense of right and wrong.

But the point is, there was no reason for her to take a call from me. Which could only mean one thing: Paige knew where Noelle was. And tonight, I was going to get her to tell me. I'd already had to lie to Headmaster Hathaway today when he'd cornered me after classes, asking why Noelle had missed the entire day. Call me crazy, but I had a feeling he didn't actually believe me when I'd told him she'd taken a mental health day and gone to Bliss Spa in the city. I had to find Noelle fast, because if he kept asking, I wasn't going to be able to keep up the "tell no one" rule for very long. And if I cracked, the kidnappers were clear on what would happen. The words "SHE DIES" were pretty much permanently emblazoned across my mind's eye.

As I stepped into the freezing cold Billings Chapel, I felt a surge of strength. This was my home turf, and they'd come in here and sullied it. Snatched away my best friend right out from under my nose. Just by telling Paige to meet me here I was reclaiming the upper ground. Showing them I would not be intimidated. That I wasn't afraid.

A loud creak sounded in the darkness to my right and I screeched, nearly jumping out of my skin.

Okay, so maybe I was a little bit afraid.

The wind howled overhead and I took a breath.

"There's a storm, you idiot," I whispered to myself. "Things in this old building are going to creak and moan. Just calm down."

I pulled out a book of matches from my coat pocket and walked to the first wall sconce near the back right pew. My ankles shook, but I stayed the course and lit the candle, then quickly walked along the wall, headed toward the pulpit at the front, lighting half a dozen more along the way.

I looked across the small chapel. The freshly waxed dark wood pews shone and the plank floors were free of grime. The soft glow of the candlelight lent a distinct warmth to the cozy room. I stood there for a moment, closed my eyes, and took a deep breath, waiting for a sense of calm to descend over me. Waiting to feel that comforting, looked-after feeling I always had here. As if the original Billings Girls were looking down on me, encouraging me. As if they were on my side.

But I felt nothing—nothing but a chill that shot through me by a stiff wind from a broken window.

I opened my eyes and sat down hard on the raised platform around the pulpit. Alone. I was totally and completely alone. And so was Noelle. She was out there somewhere, terrified, waiting for someone to come save her. I knew exactly what that felt like. That incredible sense of desperation. When I had been left to die on a deserted island in St. Barths I had started to hallucinate. Started to think I would be better off dead. Started to think no one out in the real world even cared I was gone. That depth of despair was not something I would wish upon my worst enemy, let alone my best friend.

I hugged my knees to my chest and rested my chin between them. *I'm going to find you, Noelle. Just stay strong.*

Then the wind whistled through the eaves again. Up in the rafters, a pair of crows I hadn't noticed before flapped their wings noisily, as if mocking me.

"Oh, why don't you just fly south for the winter already?" I shouted up at them.

They were wrong. Paige was going to tell me what she knew. I was going to make sure of that. This would all be over by morning.

The arched chapel door creaked open and Paige stepped inside, cursing under her breath. She shoved the door closed with some effort, blocking out the wind. I jumped to my feet, adrenaline pumping as she dusted snow off the sleeves of her black cashmere coat. Finally, she drew the gray knit cap from her auburn hair as she turned around.

"God! Could this place be more impossible to get to?" she snapped. Her stiletto-heeled boots—not exactly the best gear for hiking snow-covered hills at night—click-clacked against the floor, the sound echoing through the chapel as she walked to the center of the aisle. "I could have died out there."

There were just way too many good comebacks to that one. About Noelle potentially dying out there right now. About the number of times *I'd* almost died at her mother's hand. About how I'd like to wring her throat for all the crap she'd pulled on the island, not to mention her current crime. But I just swallowed all the words cramming my throat. I said nothing, hoping my silence and serious glare would intimidate her.

"So?" she said, turning her gloved palms out. "Let's have it."

I blinked. "Have what?"

"Your capitulation," Paige said. "That is why you called me, right?"

"My capitulation? What the hell are you talking about?" I demanded, stepping toward her. "I called you about Noelle."

"Noelle? Why? Is she here?" Paige looked around and then laughed. "Oh, this'll be good. I'd *love* to get an apology from Her Majesty. Noelle!" she sang. "Come out, come out wherever you are!"

I was so confused I actually stood there for a moment with my jaw hanging open. So much for the position of authority. I looked like the town idiot, the dumbfounded subject of the punch line.

"If this is your idea of a joke—"

"Reed, you're the one who called me, remember?" Paige replied, whipping her cell phone out of her Prada bag and checking for messages. "Now, *clearly* you've decided to give up your little Billings project, whatever that was, but *clearly* I wouldn't be here unless you wanted something in return. So what is it? What are your petty little demands?"

"My petty little . . ." I gritted my teeth together, clenched my fists, and prayed for patience. "Paige, this isn't a joke. Where the hell is Noelle?"

"She's not here?" Paige said blankly, jerking her head to look behind her. Her auburn curls twitched around her face.

A cold sense of realization washed through me. I was utterly and completely wrong. Paige had no idea where Noelle was. Had no idea she was even missing. There was no way she was a good enough actress to fake this level of cluelessness. She thought that I'd merely summoned her here to tell her I was giving up the BLS—that the lame-ass threats she and her fellow alums had made against me and my sisters had worked. This whole undertaking was pointless.

"I have to go," I said, brushing by her.

"Wait. You have *got* to be kidding me," Paige said. "That's it? You have nothing else to say to me?"

I turned on my heel to look at her, my face aflame with anger, frustration, and despair. "Yeah. The next time you're visiting the prison down in Virginia, tell your mom I said 'Hi.'"

Then I turned and stormed out into the cold, not even bothering to cover up this time. The Billings Alums didn't have Noelle. Or if they did, they hadn't told Paige about it. So who the hell had done this? And where were they keeping Noelle?

I emerged from the tree line, the stone buildings and winking lights of the Easton campus spread out below me at the bottom of the snow-covered hill, as if all were right in the world. Then I heard a jingle. My breath caught and I paused. Nothing. It was just the wind playing tricks on me. But then I heard it again. It was my phone. I was so riled up that I didn't even recognize the sound of my own phone. Biting down on my tongue, I fumbled in my pocket for my cell, nearly dropping it in the snowdrift. Snowflakes clung to my eyelashes and the wind bit at my nose as I narrowed my blurred eyes and tried to read.

THE GAME BEGINS NOW. IF YOU EVER WANT TO SEE NOELLE ALIVE AGAIN, YOU WILL HAVE TO COMPLETE FOUR ASSIGNMENTS. DO EXACTLY AS WE SAY AND TELL NO ONE. ASSIGNMENT NUMBER ONE: HAVE GRANDMOTHER LANGE SIGN A LETTER EXCUSING NOELLE FROM SCHOOL FOR THE NEXT TWO WEEKS. NO FAXING, TEXTING, OR E-MAILS ALLOWED. GRANDMOTHER LANGE MUST BE APPROACHED IN PERSON. THE LETTER MUST BE AN ORIGINAL, WITH AN ORIGINAL SIGNATURE. NO FORGERIES ACCEPTED. WE'LL BE WATCHING YOU.

My lungs completely emptied out, ice-cold dread seeping through my body. I glanced over my shoulder at the snow-laden trees. Could Paige have sent this text? She'd had her phone out when I'd walked away from her. Maybe she *was* screwing with me. If someone was watching me right now, it had to be her. She was the only one out here.

Or was she?

I closed my eyes against a crippling stab of terror and told myself to breathe. No one else was out here. No one even knew where I was other than Josh. The kidnappers were just trying to scare me. And I was not going to let them.

When I opened my eyes again and looked around, all I saw were trees, snow, and the campus below. Paige could not have sent the text. I had to go with my gut. The girl knew nothing. She knew less than nothing.

A gust of wind knocked me sideways and I reached back, pulling my hood over my head. Huddling against the wide trunk of an old elm tree, I bent over the phone and read the message again. This made no sense. Okay, yes, I understood why the kidnapper wanted Noelle excused from school. If she wasn't, the faculty and administration would get suspicious and start asking questions—especially at Easton, where they had been trained by experience to be severely paranoid. But why would they want me to get a note from Grandma Lange? Noelle had two parents, alive and well. Shouldn't they be the ones to get her excused from school?

I gritted my teeth. It didn't matter whether it made sense. It was my task, and I had to complete it. Noelle's life was on the line.

I put my phone away, ducked my head, and started the long trudge back to campus, trying all the way not to look back over my shoulder. Trying to ignore the sinking sense that someone was, in fact, watching my every step.

REVENGE

"Reed! Oh my God! You have to stop them!"

Amberly Carmichael accosted me the second I speed-walked through the door to Pemberly, and as tense as I was, my heart practically vaulted up my throat and out my mouth.

"Stop who?" I said, clenching my fists to keep from bursting into flames or tears or just screaming my head off. I inhaled slowly then exhaled, trying to calm my frayed, paranoid nerves.

"Them!" Amberly threw her hand out toward the lounge. That was when I saw that she was not alone. Kiki Rosen, Astrid Chou, Vienna Clarke, and Tiffany Goubourne were all seated on the old, fading brocade couches, coats off, Coffee Carma cups on the coffee table before them. "They're totally plotting against Noelle."

My head went light as I stepped into the room. *Join the club.*

Tiffany rolled her brown eyes toward the ceiling. "We're not plotting against her. We just want our revenge," she said with a conspiratorial smile.

The door slammed behind me and I jumped.

"Revenge on whom?" Ivy asked. She'd just come in from outside and was now hovering behind me in her white coat. She tugged her black leather gloves from her fingers and gave me a questioning look.

"Noelle," Astrid replied, popping her gum.

Ivy laughed, her eyes bright. "I'm *so very* in." She walked over to the nearest couch and sat down next to Tiffany.

My stomach twisted itself up like a cats' cradle, changing formations every two seconds. I lowered myself into an empty chair, weak from the many scares of the past ten minutes. "Revenge for what?"

"For that ridiculous prank she played on us last night," Vienna said, like it was so obvious. She flicked her thick, highlighted hair over her shoulder and crossed her skinny-jeans-clad legs at the knee. "I mean, I practically had a heart attack."

"I think I *did* have a heart attack," Amberly said, touching her fingertips to her neck. She walked up behind my chair. "See? My pulse is *still* elevated."

"Then I don't get why you won't let us use you," Kiki said, lifting her legs and dropping her feet, one at a time, atop the coffee table. Her heavy black boots each came down with a bang. The coffee cups jumped.

"Because! I think what you're planning is unusually cruel and besides . . . it's Noelle," Amberly said, flouncing around my chair and sitting down on the arm.

"So you're just afraid of Noelle," Astrid said. "You're a patsy, is what you're saying."

The other girls snickered.

"I'm not afraid of her," Amberly pouted, sliding her long blond hair through her fingers over and over again. "It's just that she's been one of my best friends for, like, ever."

Tiffany and I exchanged a look. We both knew Noelle didn't think of Amberly as a friend so much as a lap dog.

"I don't want to do this to her," Amberly added.

"Do what, exactly?" I asked wearily.

Tiffany sat forward at this. "We were thinking that when she gets back, we should tell her that Amberly's in the hospital. That the whole ordeal fried her delicate nerves and she had to be medicated."

"Vienna's boyfriend's brother is interning at Easton Hospital and he said he could get us an empty room and hook up some machines to beep and stuff. Make it look real," Astrid added.

"We could even put her in a straitjacket," Kiki said with a smirk, eyeing Amberly. "That would be awesome."

Amberly paled. My face screwed up in disgust. "That's sick!"

"And scaring the shit out of all of us by pretending to be kidnapped is, what? Normal behavior?" Vienna snapped.

"You guys, just no. You can't do this," I said, standing up so fast I almost knocked Amberly over. "You don't know . . . you don't understand. . . ."

"Understand what, Reed?" Astrid asked. "That Noelle thinks she can get away with anything? I thought we were all equals now. If we get her back it's like—"

"It's like proving that we are," Kiki said. "Equals, I mean."

I paced around the back of the chair, my pulse pounding in my ears, my very hair follicles sizzling with anger and fear and frustration. They had no idea where Noelle really was right now, what she was really going through. This whole thing was so wrong, so petty, such a huge, stupid waste of time. Why was I even here? Why was I even listening to this when I had more important things to do?

Like saving Noelle's life.

But I couldn't say any of this. Couldn't tell them what I was really thinking or feeling. The frustration was such agony, I wanted to punch something.

I glanced over at them and saw that Ivy was watching me very carefully. Almost like she could read my mind, or at least my mood. I grabbed on to that glance, held on to it for dear life, silently begged her to just help me.

"Reed's right. It's no good," Ivy said.

"What?" Vienna blurted, crossing her arms over her chest. "I thought *you'd* jump on the bandwagon like your pants were on fire."

"I can see why you'd think that, but I don't know," Ivy replied, looking me right in the eye. "Noelle had to go home for a family emergency, right?" she asked.

I nodded mutely, unable to speak past the lump in my throat.

"So isn't it kind of cruel to attack her right when she gets back?" Ivy asked. "I mean, who knows what she might be dealing with right now? We're supposed to be her friends."

I could tell it took some effort for her to mention herself among Noelle's friends, and I was beyond grateful for it.

"Yeah, but—"

"Besides, I hate to point out the obvious, you guys, but your prank kind of sucks," Ivy said, standing and gathering her things. "I mean, we all know Amberly's a delicate flower, but going catatonic in a mental ward because of a prank? Noelle would never believe that, even if you had Dr. Phil come in here and swear to it."

"It's not *that* bad," Astrid muttered, sitting back in her chair, her cheeks pink. Clearly it was her idea.

"Yeah. It is," Ivy said bluntly. "You guys give me a couple of days and I promise I'll come up with something way better. Something we can pull on her later when she least expects it," she said, giving me a steady look.

Thank you, I said with my eyes.

She gave me a small smile in return. She was doing this for me, not for Noelle. But either way, I didn't care.

"Agreed?" I asked the crowd, my voice a croak.

"Agreed!" Amberly chirped, jumping to her feet.

The girls all looked at one another. "Agreed," they said reluctantly.

Relief flooded my veins. I had never loved Ivy more.

CAT BURGLAR

"Wow. So, you've done this before," Josh joked as he stuck his head through the basement window of Hull Hall. I had just shimmied through the narrow space and dropped to the floor without hesitation, landing easily and soundlessly on my feet.

"Kind of," I replied.

I'd done it last fall when Noelle, Ariana Osgood, Kiran Hayes, and Taylor Bell had dared me to as a way to prove myself to Billings. I'd done it again with Dash McCafferty when we'd been trying to figure out who'd killed Thomas Pearson. And I'd done it a few times last month with my friends, when we'd held the first secret meetings leading up to the initiation of the Billings Literary Society.

If the whole Ivy League thing didn't work out, I was going to have to consider a career as a cat burglar.

Josh turned around and slid through the window feetfirst, his long legs dangling for a moment before he got up the guts to drop down.

When he hit the cement floor, his knees buckled and he fell into me. I caught him awkwardly with my arms around his back and his face pressed into my shoulder.

"Well. That was emasculating," he joked, his green eyes shining as he straightened up.

I smiled, giving him a placating pat on the shoulder. "No worries," I whispered. "I still love you." We both blushed. We didn't throw the word "love" around lightly or too often. "Come on. Let's get this over with."

Together we crept over to the door. Josh held up a hand—taking the lead in an attempt to regain his manliness, I guessed—and opened it himself, wincing when it let out a loud creak. He peered into the hall then motioned for me to follow him. I smiled and shook my head at the huge streak of white paint across the back of his right pant leg. I'd told him to dress in all black, but I could never trust my artist boyfriend to wear any piece of clothing that wasn't marred by paint.

If someone was, in fact, always watching me, they could have spotted both of us by a country mile with that streak glowing in the dark. A chill shot straight through me and the smile dropped from my lips. At least now we were safely inside, away from prying eyes.

The back stone stairwell was even colder than the air outside, and we quickly raced up the steps, taking them two at a time. Once in the main hall, we stayed close to the wall until we got to the bottom of the wide oak staircase. Josh looked both ways and nodded. We flew up to the second floor, sprinting noisily down the hall to the headmaster's office at the very end.

"Hang on," Josh whispered, placing his hand on the old brass doorknob. He rested his ear against the thick wooden door and listened.

"No one's in there," I said. "It's after midnight."

"I don't know about you, but Double H has always struck me as a workaholic," Josh said. Double H was the nickname we had for Headmaster Hathaway, Sawyer and Graham's dad, who had taken over as the head of the school at the beginning of the semester. When Josh, Graham, and Sawyer had been at St. James Academy together, Mr. Hathaway had been the headmaster there, too, so Josh had more experience with the man than I did. And he had a point. The man had "work is my life" written all over him.

Slowly, carefully, Josh opened the door and looked inside. The outer office was dark, so we slipped in and closed the door behind us. Luckily, the entryway to the headmaster's office, which was directly across the room, was open too. Moonlight shone in through the tall, wide windows.

"All clear," Josh said.

"You've seen too many cop movies." I elbowed him with a smirk, trying to cover up my nerves. Yanking out the chair behind the secretary's desk, I booted up her computer and waited for the Easton Academy home page to load.

"How are you going to get in?" Josh asked, leaning one hand on the desk.

"I still have Lance Reagan's secret code," I told him.

"Lance Reagan's what now?" he asked.

I glanced at him over my shoulder. "I thought all the Ketlar boys had it."

Josh's brow knit. "I've never even heard of it," he said, pouting.

"Oh," I said, blushing. "Sorry."

"Can it get you into any computer on campus?" Josh asked.

"Yep." I nodded.

"How did *you* get it?" Josh asked, standing up straight and crossing his arms over his chest.

My face burned and I turned my attention to the computer. Josh would not like hearing about me and Dash sneaking in here alone, nor about the fact that Dash had shared this boys-only secret with me and not him. Especially considering Josh and I had broken up just a few months afterward when he'd caught me and Dash kissing at the Legacy. We'd been drugged at the time, but still. It wasn't a favorite memory for either of us.

"I'm just that connected," I said casually, my fingers flying over the keyboard. I hit enter and the computer beeped ominously.

INVALID PASSWORD. PLEASE RE-ENTER YOUR PASSWORD NOW.

My heart sunk to my toes. "Crap. They must have figured it out and blocked it."

"Let's try Hathaway's computer," Josh suggested, moving toward the other office.

"Why? What makes you think you can get into his?"

Josh settled in behind the wide desk while I stood tentatively in the doorway. "He's a dad. Dads always use their kids' birthdays as passwords."

Huh. I wondered if my dad did that. And if so, did he use mine or my brother, Scott's?

"And what? You know Sawyer and Graham's birthdays?" I asked. A few embers glowed in the big, stone fireplace on the far side of the room, and I got a chill as I remembered being interrogated by Headmaster Cromwell in front of that fireplace earlier this school year, on the night Cheyenne Martin was killed.

"No. But I know Jen's," Josh said.

My heart twisted. Jen Hathaway had been Josh's girlfriend at St. James.

Josh hit enter. There was another ugly beep.

"Damn," he said. "Didn't work."

"Maybe he's got the boys' birthdays on his paper calendar." I nudged the rolling chair he sat in with my hip so I could flip through the blotter-style calendar atop the headmaster's desk. There were all kinds of appointments listed—meetings with the board every Monday, a founder's luncheon in March, a budget meeting every month—but no birthdays.

"Nothing personal anywhere," I groused.

"Told you he's a workaholic," Josh said.

Downstairs, a door slammed. We both gasped and my hand flew to my mouth.

"What else could it be?" Josh whispered urgently, his fingers poised over the keyboard.

Suddenly an idea popped into my mind. An idea that was way too morbid to work, but it was all I had. "What about the day Jen died?" I whispered.

Josh looked at me in almost an accusatory way. Like he was ashamed that my brain could even go there.

"Do you know when it was?" I said, ignoring his look. "Sometime last summer. . . ."

"I know," he said quietly.

"Just try it," I hissed.

He did. His fingers hovered for a second above the enter key, but when he finally hit it, the welcome screen came to life.

"It worked. I can't believe it worked," he said. "Hathaway's even more twisted than you are."

There was another slam. Closer this time. Josh and I froze. Then came the distinct sound of whistling, and the squeak of unoiled wheels moving closer and closer and closer. For a split second there was silence. And then the door to the outer office opened.

"Shit," Josh whispered.

He hit the floor and jammed himself in under the desk. I couldn't move. Terror took hold as the whistling echoed eerily off the high ceilings in the outer office.

"Reed!" Josh whispered, groping for my hand. He yanked on my fingers and I dove down, my knees slamming into the hardwood floor. I whimpered in pain as I curled into a ball and crammed in next to him.

Janitor, Josh mouthed as we heard the sound of a garbage can being slammed against another while it was being emptied.

The whistling grew louder. The janitor was coming in. His feet shuffled along the floor and he let out a groan as he lifted the headmaster's garbage can. He walked out into the secretary's office with it, knocked it against the larger can, then came back and replaced it. Throughout this entire enterprise, I didn't breathe once. Josh's hand clutched mine so hard I thought he was going to dislocate my fingers. Then the outer office door closed, the wheels squeaked again, and the whistling faded away.

"Oh. My. God," I whispered.

Josh nodded, his face millimeters from mine. "Let's get this info already and get the hell out of here."

We crawled out and I stood up, taking a deep breath. Quickly, I brought up the student information folder and found Noelle's file. In it was the contact information for her parents, as well as all three of her living grandparents. Noelle's grandmother, Lenora Lange, was listed as an alumna of Easton, and also of Billings House. I scrolled to her address and phone number and my heart completely stopped.

"Sonofa—" Josh exhaled over my shoulder.

Grandmother Lange lived in Paris, France.

FRIEND WITH BENEFITS

I stared at the bank balance on my computer on Friday morning, wondering if what was left of my Billings Fund money would be enough to cover a round-trip ticket to Paris, which was, of course, the least of my worries. If I was going to do this, I was going to have to get off campus, which required an excuse and a pass. And even if I did manage to get that, I was going to have to find a way to get to the airport, and a way to get to Mrs. Lange after that. Not to mention I had to figure out how the hell I was going to explain to the old woman—whom I'd never met—that I'd just flown across the Atlantic to get an excuse note for Noelle, when I could have simply gone to her parents in New York, and when I had no idea where Noelle herself was.

My head dropped and my forehead pressed into the keyboard as I moaned in desperation. If only I knew someone in France, preferably someone who knew Noelle and her family. Where was Kiran Hayes these days? Didn't models spend, like, 75 percent of their time in Paris? I lifted my head again, a twitter of hope inside my heart. But then, if I called Kiran, I'd have to explain. And she would completely freak out if she knew Noelle was missing. Besides, I wasn't supposed to tell anyone. What I really needed was someone who would just do this for me, no questions asked.

Someone European.

I laughed mournfully at my own silly turn of thoughts. Like I, Reed Brennan from Croton, Pennsylvania, was supertight with anyone, anywhere in Europe. And then it hit me like an arrow to the chest.

Upton Giles.

My very fingertips tingled and I bit my bottom lip in excitement. I could call Upton. Upton would do anything for me. He'd both said and proven so more than once. He may not have been in France, but he was in England, which was a hell of a lot closer to Paris than Easton, Connecticut.

I glanced at the clock. It was 7:15 a.m. here, which meant it was 12:15 p.m. there. Could I possibly be lucky enough to find him in his dorm room? It was worth a shot.

I quickly opened up Skype and dialed Upton's number. It rang a few times while I looked at the hold screen and then, all of a sudden, he was there. Smiling, shirtless, Upton Giles leaned over his desk as he hit the keyboard to answer my call.

"Reed! What a fantastic surprise!"

I got an extreme close-up of his bare chest as he sat down at his desk, and then his gorgeous face was in full view again. Already, I was blushing. I may have been completely committed to Josh now, but that didn't mean I was immune to Upton's world-renowned hotness.

"Hi, Upton. It's good to see you. But is there a reason you're shirtless at noon?" I joked.

He laughed that carefree Upton-y laugh. "Do I offend?" he said, opening his arms wide.

I blushed even harder, remembering exactly what it felt like to be in those arms, leaning against that chest, listening to the beat of his heart.

Okay, Reed. Focus. This is not about that right now. This is about Noelle.

"Not at all," I said. "But Upton, I'm actually calling because I need a favor. A huge, important favor."

Upton's expression grew serious. "What is it?"

"Is there any possible way you could go to Paris?" I asked, biting my lip again, this time out of extreme doubt. "Like, today?"

Upton laughed while I stayed deadly silent. "Wait. You're serious."

"There's this kind of a scavenger hunt thing going on at school," I said, making things up on the fly, "and the prize is . . . well, it's something I really want. But there's something I'm supposed to get from Paris," I told him.

"What is it?" Upton asked.

"I have to get a note from Noelle's grandmother excusing her from school for the next two weeks," I said. "And I need it overnighted to me."

There was no way he was ever going to buy this. The whole thing

sounded so ridiculous, even to my own ears, that I half expected him
to ask what drugs I was experimenting with.

"Why would *you* need to get *that*?" he asked. "Sounds more like
something Noelle would have to get."

"Well, we're a team," I told him, surprised at how easily the lies
were rolling off my tongue. "The two of us."

"Oh. Okay, then," he said, lifting one shoulder. "Why not? I could
go for some authentic croque monsieur. Plus, I worship Lenora. She's
a total minx, that one."

"You know Noelle's grandmother?" I asked, surprised.

"Of course I do," Upton said, clearly surprised. "Our families go
way back, remember?"

"So you think she'd be okay with this?" I asked.

"Are you kidding?" Upton said. "Woman's got a latent wild streak
that burns brighter than Noelle's does. But Noelle could have told you
all this. Is she even there?"

"Not right now," I said, swallowing at a sudden tightness in my
throat. "I came up with the idea to call you on my own."

"Oh, okay. Well, tell her it's done. And if she has any messages to
relay to Grandma, have her text me."

I swallowed again, my throat now filled with a heavy mix of grati-
tude, guilt, and fear. Noelle wasn't going to be texting anyone any
time soon. She might never see her grandmother again. That was,
unless this crazy plan of mine worked. "Upton, thank you so much.
Really. You're a lifesaver."

"I don't know about that," he said. "But this'll be fun."

"Whatever you say," I replied with a grin. "Thanks, Upton."

Just then there was a quick rap on my door and it started to open.

"No worries, Reed. Cheers!" Upton said as Josh walked into my room. Josh took one look at the screen and stopped in his tracks. My face burned brighter than the winter sun outside my window.

"Bye!" I replied as I slapped the laptop closed.

I turned around in my chair, my heart pounding in my temples and my palms slick with sweat. Josh looked at me quizzically. How much of Upton's half-naked body had he actually seen?

"Who was that?" he asked.

"No one. Just an old friend," I replied. "He lives in England and he knows the Langes, so he's going to help us get the excuse note."

"Oh," Josh said, his voice flat. "That's good, then."

"Good? It's incredible. Now I don't have to find a way to get to Paris and back today. Not to mention a way to pay for it." I got up and tried to go about getting my things together as if everything was normal, but Josh was still staring at me.

"Yeah. I'd say that's definitely a plus," he said eventually. "So, ready for breakfast?"

"Yeah," I replied, avoiding eye contact as I grabbed my coat and slipped by him out the door. I glanced back at my computer, as if Upton was going to be sitting there, shirtless and waving at me. "Let's get out of here."

MISSION ACCOMPLISHED

I sat on the stone bench outside the Easton student post office on Saturday morning. I kicked at the snow, waiting for the FedEx truck to arrive. Upton had texted me to let me know my package would be here, but it couldn't come fast enough. Noelle had already missed two days of school with no explanation. What if Headmaster Hathaway had called her parents? What if he was calling them right this very moment? I imagined a helicopter blowing all the snow off the trees as it landed in the center of the quad, and Noelle's handsome father stepping out, the picture of concern and determination, ready to consult with the FBI task force, ready to do anything and spare no expense to find his daughter.

Which would, of course, make it look like I'd broken the whole "don't tell her parents" rule. Yeah. If this didn't work, I was screwed.

A frigid breeze stung my face and I tugged my scarf up over my nose. I should have gone inside the post office and warmed up, but I wanted to see the truck arrive. I needed to be there when it pulled up.

After what seemed like an Antarctic eternity, I heard the rumble of an engine. A white truck came around the bend, its sides caked with muddy snow splatters. It ground to a stop behind the post office and the driver yanked on the emergency brake, leaving the engine idling. After he'd gathered his deliveries from the back, I ran for the door of the post office and held it open for him.

Please just don't let there have been any mix-ups, I thought silently as I pressed my lips into a tight smile. *Please, please, please let it be there.*

"Thanks," the delivery guy said, eyeing me with surprise. I guess not a lot of private school girls had held doors open for him in the past.

"No problem."

I stood on my toes, trying to see the names on his armful of packages. He held them tighter to his chest and shot me an admonishing glance.

Biting back my frustration, I trailed him over to the mail window. Mrs. Morrison, the most elderly of all the elderly mail people employed by Easton Academy, groaned as she pushed herself off her stool and placed her Sudoku puzzle and pencil down behind the counter. I knew the protocol. Mrs. Morrison had to log everything in first before my package could be signed over to me. If there was, in fact, a package for me.

I bounced up and down on my toes in an attempt to bring some feeling back into them. Also because I couldn't have stayed still if a sumo wrestler had walked into the room, thrown me to the floor, and sat down on my chest.

The FedEx guy placed five packages down on the countertop—two boxes and three flat letters. My heart seized up when I spied Upton's scrawled handwriting on one of the envelopes. I clutched my gloved hands together, doing all I could do to keep from snatching it.

"Do you mind, miss?" the delivery dude asked, glancing down at me. "You're a little close."

"Sorry," I said, mortified. I backed away and waited for him and Mrs. Morrison to complete the transaction, then gave him an apologetic smile as he left the office.

"Here you go, Miss Brennan," Mrs. Morrison croaked, her voice hoarse from about sixty years of cigarette smoking. She pushed the letter across the small countertop to me and I quickly signed the slip. "What is it that's got you so bouncy? A love letter?" she asked, raising one eyebrow slyly.

"Something like that," I replied. I turned around, tearing into the envelope like a rabid dog. Inside was a sealed, cream-colored envelope with the words "Headmaster Hathaway, Easton Academy" written in flowing script across the front, along with a note from Upton. The whole package smelled of lavender. It wafted up from the envelope, filling my senses and enveloping me like a hug. Somehow it made me feel calm, and a smile lit my face as I unfolded Upton's note.

Mission accomplished, beautiful. I do so love a visit with Lenora. She's an incredible woman. I told her she'd like you and she said

she hopes to meet you one day. I think you two have a lot in com-
mon. Hope you win the scavenger hunt.

    Love,

    Upton

I smiled and tucked the note into my bag, wondering what on Earth I could possibly have in common with Mrs. Lange.

"Thanks, Mrs. Morrison!" I trilled, feeling momentarily peppy now that I had the note in my possession. She lifted a hand, her eyes already trained on her puzzle. I took a deep breath and headed back out into the cold. Upton may have accomplished his part of the mission, but I still had to complete mine.

I quickly trudged across the snow-laced stone walkway to Hull Hall and strode right through the front door. My boots left wet treads on the hardwood floor. The closer I got to the headmaster's office on the second level, the faster I moved. I was so eager to get this over with I could barely breathe. I tried to quell my nerves as I passed through the deserted outer office. It seemed the headmaster had given his secretary the day off.

The door to Mr. Hathaway's private space was open. He sat in a high-backed chair by the fire, going over some papers, his feet up on the ornate marble-topped coffee table. I knocked on the open door and walked in, my throat dry. Even if this somehow worked and Mr. Hathaway accepted this excuse note, how were the kidnappers going to know? Was I supposed to text them back and tell them I'd finished the task? But I supposed that was a hurdle I could jump once I'd cleared this one.

"Hello, Reed," Mr. Hathaway said, laying his stack of papers down and placing his feet on the floor. "What brings you to my office on a Saturday morning?"

I strode toward him across the Oriental rug, trying to appear as if everything was fine and normal. "Noelle asked me to give you this."

Headmaster Hathaway eyed the envelope for a moment before plucking it from my grasp. He picked up a silver letter opener from the coffee table and slit it open with such precision it barely even made a ripping noise. The swift action made me gulp.

Please let this work, I thought again, clutching my gloved hands together in front of me as his eyes flicked over the page. *Please, please, please let this work*. I had a feeling I was going to be doing a lot of silent begging in the immediate, foreseeable future.

Finally Mr. Hathaway cleared his throat. He refolded the letter and tucked it back into its envelope. Hours seemed to pass before he looked up at me and spoke.

"Kindly tell Miss Lange that, in the future, she is to deliver her excuses to me herself," he said.

Then he turned back to his paperwork and crossed his ankles on the table once more. I hesitated. What, exactly, did that mean? Was she excused from classes or not?

"Um, Mr. Hathaway? I'm sorry to bother you, but I just—"

"Don't worry, Reed," he replied, lifting a dismissive hand, a silver pen clasped between two fingers. "Noelle is excused until her family no longer needs her."

Relief rushed through me so fast my knees almost buckled. "Oh.

Okay. Thanks. Thanks, Mr. Hathaway!" I said a bit overenthusiasti-
cally. "I guess I'll just . . . see ya!"

Then I tore out of there, slamming the door behind me in my zeal,
realizing too late that it had been open when I'd arrived. But who
cared? I ran down the stairs to the first floor and out into the sunshine, feeling as if I'd just been granted a new chance at life. But at
the bottom of the outdoor stairs I paused. I still had no idea how I was
going to let the kidnappers know I'd completed their insane assignment.

"Hey, Reed!"

I looked up to find Kiki and Astrid striding toward me. Kiki's white
knit cap almost covered her pink-streaked hair, and Astrid wore
bright green earmuffs to match her green and purple plaid coat.

"Hey, guys," I said with an awkward smile. As much as I loved my
friends, this wasn't the best moment for company. I felt an almost
primal need to be alone so I could figure out what to do next.

"Come with us!" Kiki said, tucking her arm through mine.

"Come where?" I asked, trying to figure out a way to pull away from
her without seeming rude.

"We're going to Coffee Carma to load up on caffeine for a full day
of research," Astrid said, hemming me in on the other side.

My heart thumped with that awful feeling that I'd forgotten something. "Research? For what?" I asked.

"That English assignment?" Kiki said, tucking her chin and looking at me like I'd just started speaking backward. "A fictional account
of a day in the life of your favorite classical author?"

Right. That little thing. Leave it to Mrs. Carr to figure out a way to mix creative writing with extensive research with fiction reading and toss it all at us with a psychotic deadline. How the hell was I ever going to have the time or the brain space to work on something like that?

"Have you picked your author yet?" Astrid asked, blowing a purple gum bubble. "I'm doing Mary Shelley. I'd just love to imagine a day in the life of *that* twisted mind."

"No. Not yet," I replied as they steered me toward Mitchell Hall. The largest building on campus, Mitchell housed the Great Room, the solarium with its Coffee Carma counter, the art cemetery, and several meeting rooms and parlors. I glanced over my shoulder, looking for an escape. "I just . . . don't know." It was next to impossible to speak like a normal person while plotting to get away from them and panicking about the kidnappers at the same time. "Maybe I'll think of something once I've got a cinnamon chip scone in me," I heard myself say.

"Oh! A cinnamon chip scone!" Astrid said, hugging me a bit closer to her side. "Brilliant! That's why you're our fearless leader."

Fearless? Hardly. Leader? I definitely didn't feel like one. Finally I gave up on an escape plan and simply allowed them to drag me across campus. I decided that I would hit the bathroom when we got inside and try to reply-text to the last text I'd been sent. What else could I do? I had to let my evil puppeteer know I was ready for my next assignment.

As soon as the door to Mitchell Hall slammed behind us, my phone beeped. My heart launched into my throat, a sensation that I seemed to feel ten times a day lately, but could not get used to.

"I'll catch up with you," I said, pausing near the door.

"We'll get in line!" Kiki said, tugging her hat off as they made their way down the hall toward the bustling conservatory. "Oh! Maybe I'll get a chocolate chip scone."

"It's only fair. Equal time for all manner of chips, I say," Astrid agreed.

Envying their carefree banter, I whipped out my phone. I had one new text. Fingers trembling, I somehow managed to open it.

ASSIGNMENT ONE COMPLETE. GOOD WORK. STAND BY FOR FURTHER INSTRUCTIONS.

I looked out the slim window in the door, but there was nothing. No one. Just a couple of guys walking from Ketlar to the library, and a pack of freshman girls headed to the gym. A chill went down my spine. Apparently the kidnappers had been telling the truth. They were watching me.

I just wanted to know how.

STARES AND GLARES

In 1903, Ida M. Tarbell published an article that launched the reform journalism trend and had great ramifications on big business in America. What was the article titled? What was it about? Discuss the impact reform journalism had on government regulations and business practices in the Unites States.

I read the question, trying to make the words stick in my mind.

Ramifications. Ram-if-ick-a-shunnns. That's a funny word.

I snorted in the back of my throat. Cooper Banks, the guy in the next desk, and the only dude on campus who insisted on wearing a tie to class every day, shot me an annoyed look and continued to scribble his essay answer in his tiny, psycho-killer style scrawl.

I looked down at my paper. Each of the first three questions had answers, but I'd written them in huge, loopy script, trying to fill up the space with as few words as possible. I was so going to fail this thing.

My eyes started to close for the ten billionth time since I'd sat down to take this exam. I'd been up all night, staring at the clock, waiting for my next set of instructions, which had never come, and now I was paying the price. I shook my head, gave my cheeks a quick pinch, and sat up straight, but nothing worked. It was like a team of tiny strong men were clinging to my upper lashes, using all their weight to pull them back down. Maybe if I just closed them for one, tiny second. . . .

Suddenly my hand hit the desk, my watch smacking against the wood with a noise loud enough to wake the dead. A couple of people around me flinched. I looked at Constance, who was seated to my left, and tried for a "silly me" smile. She scowled a very un-Constance-like scowl, and leaned over her paper, but she wasn't working on her test. The exam paper—which was completed, I noticed with chagrin—had been pushed off to the side, and she was now jotting down notes on a list entitled "V-Day Dance."

My face felt hot and I looked away. Clearly Constance was on the planning committee for the dance, something she would have announced to me with her particular brand of hyper excitement if we'd still been on speaking terms. We hadn't spoken since our fight in the cafeteria over her not getting into the Billings Literary Society. Not one word. And I seriously missed her.

From the corner of my eye I saw someone at the door. I flinched when I saw that it was Headmaster Hathaway. He was just standing there, watching me. And when he saw me look, he didn't turn away.

Now my face was on fire. What was he doing out there? Spying on me? I forced myself to look at my paper but couldn't get my brain to focus on the question. Not with Double H staring me down. Then I glanced up at the door again, and he was gone.

Okay. Deep breath. He's probably just doing the rounds. He wasn't looking at you, he was just . . . looking at the room.

I read the question yet again. Maybe all this weirdness would keep me awake.

In 1903, Ida M. Tarbell . . .

Instantly, my eyes started to close again.

Then something beeped.

My head popped up and my hand was in my bag before I registered the fact that everyone around me was getting up from their seats, gathering their things, handing in their exam papers at the front of the room. It was the end-of-class tone that had sounded. Not my cell phone. I had fallen fast asleep. There was even a spot of drool on my test paper. My heart sunk to my toes. I looked down at the screen on my phone, just in case, but there were no new messages. Aside from the usual texts from the other Billings Girls and some check-ins from my brother, Scott, there had been nothing since Saturday morning. It was as if the kidnappers were enjoying keeping me in the dark, torturing me.

Did that mean they were torturing Noelle, too?

Constance was just getting up from her chair. As she picked up her V-Day dance list I saw that among the "to-do's" were "Call the caterer" and "Have London confirm napkins and favors."

"Are you planning the Valentine's Day dance?" I blurted.

Constance turned to me with a scowl. "Yeah. I am."

"That's cool," I said, my heart pounding.

"Yeah, well, I read this article that said that when all your friends dump you, it's good to throw yourself into something new. You know, as a distraction from your misery," Constance said in an acerbic tone.

I cleared my throat. The fact that I'd made her sound like that made me feel like ralphing. "Is London helping too?"

"Yeah. She's all into it," Constance replied. "We've been hanging out a lot since you decided to ostracize us."

She adjusted the strap of her bag on her shoulder and I felt her itching to leave. My pulse raced. I felt like the parents in one of those kidnap movies, when the FBI agent tells them to say anything to keep the kidnapper on the phone so they can trace the call. I was so stunned and excited that she'd talked to me for this long, I just wanted to keep her talking.

"Is Missy doing it too?" I asked, deciding not to acknowledge all the accusations.

"Missy? Please. Like she'd get involved in anything that might bring people joy," Constance said with a laugh. I laughed too. And for a moment, just a moment, things were the way they used to be.

Then something in her eyes changed, as if she realized she was speaking to the devil. She stood up straight and the scowl was back on. "I gotta go."

"Constance—"

But she was already down the aisle and I suddenly felt a hulking presence behind me.

"Miss Brennan?"

Mr. Barber's voice sent an unpleasant sizzle of warmth across my shoulders and down my back. I turned to face him. His dark eyes traveled over the half-empty test page on my desk, and his lips pursed ever so slightly.

"Ida M. Tarbell is not our favorite subject, I see," he said, his bow tie bobbing up and down over his Adam's apple as he spoke. He lifted the test sheet and looked down at it over the top of his new, gold-framed glasses.

"I'm sorry," I muttered. "I just . . . I haven't been sleeping well lately."

"Or perhaps you've been spending too much time texting and Twittering and whatever else it is your sad generation does on those contraptions all day long," he said, glancing derisively at my phone, which I still clutched in my hand.

My face burning, I shoved the phone back into my bag and yanked the strap off the back of the chair. It got snagged three times and finally I pulled so hard I almost knocked the chair over. Mr. Barber calmly reached out to steady the furniture, closing his eyes and taking a long, slow breath. I could practically hear his silent prayer for patience.

"Maybe I could . . . uh . . . do an extra-credit assignment?" I said.

"See me after class tomorrow," he replied, turning around and tossing my paper onto his desk.

"Okay. I will. Thanks."

I couldn't get out of there fast enough. I slid past him for the door, shoving my arms into my coat as I went, and found Lorna Gross hovering outside, waiting for me. Her long, dark hair was back in a messy bun and she wore a rhinestone headband just behind her ears. Her gray cashmere sweater was adorned with glittery snowflakes and she wore about four strands of pearls. Lorna used to copy her style right out of her BFF Missy Thurber's closet, but lately she had started to take on a look all her own, and even though it was something I could never pull off, it worked for her.

"What was that all about?" Lorna asked as she tugged on her heather gray coat and donned a pair of furry earmuffs.

"I didn't exactly finish my test," I replied, starting down the hall.

Lorna rolled her eyes and scoffed as she sidestepped a couple of senior guys who were barreling down the center of the hallway, oblivious to the world. "Who did? Ten essay questions in less than an hour? *Maybe* if he let us use our laptops."

"Really?" I asked as I pushed open the door. I felt a slight surge of hope. Perhaps I wasn't in *such* bad shape. But how many questions had I managed to answer before I started to nod off? Four? Five? I swallowed back a sour taste in the back of my throat as I realized it was probably more like three.

"Yeah. Don't worry. I'm sure you'll get an A," Lorna said, pushing open the front door of the class building with both hands. "You're Reed Brennan."

The comment actually brought tears to my eyes. Was I mourning over the straight-A student I used to be, or feeling guilty because I wasn't living up to her image of me? I had no idea. Either way, I clearly needed some sleep.

"So . . . everyone's wondering. Are we going to have another meeting of the literary society any time soon?" Lorna asked as we descended the steps. They were covered with salt to keep the ice at bay, and our shoes made crunching sounds as we walked. Part of me wanted to shush her. It was a secret society after all. But that was the beauty of calling it a literary society. We could talk about it in public with no fear of spoiling our secret.

But the very thought of the society brought a heavy weight down on my shoulders—the weight of yet another responsibility. I wished I could just put it off until I'd found Noelle, but it had been days since we met—prank meeting notwithstanding—and since none of my Billings Literary Society sisters knew that anything was wrong, they were all still flush with the newness and excitement of our secret endeavor.

"Yeah, actually. I was going to call one for tonight," I said, seeing my dream of crashing into my bed being pushed further and further away.

"Yeah?" Lorna said excitedly, giving a little jump from the bottom stair to the cobblestone walkway. Her enthusiasm brought a smile to my face, briefly anyway.

I nodded. "I'll send out the e-mail after lunch."

"Cool," Lorna said, grinning. "I think it's so awesome that you did all this, Reed. It would have sucked if the whole Billings thing had just died because the dorm got torn down."

"Thanks," I said, a flutter of pride masking my sadness for a moment. Part of me wondered what, exactly, she meant by "the whole Billings thing." I thought most people just saw Billings as a cool place to live, but clearly it meant more to Lorna than that—just like it did to me—which made me like her more.

Lorna took a deep breath of the crisp winter air and squinted across the quad. "Who's that guy with Ivy?" she asked.

I followed her gaze and saw that Ivy was standing near the library steps with the shaved-headed, leather-coat-wearing dude I had come to refer to in my mind as Tattoo Guy, due to the extremely intricate tattoo on the back of his neck. I had seen them together the month before, having an early-morning snowball fight on campus. She and Josh had still been together at the time, and I remembered thinking that she was acting kind of flirty with Tattoo Guy. Inappropriately flirty. And now, here he was again, and they seemed to be having some kind of intense conversation. Ivy gestured angrily with her hands, while he had his own hands stuffed under his armpits, looking like he was about to explode.

"That guy does *not* go here," Lorna said, wrinkling her nose.

"No. He definitely does not."

There was an odd, twisting sensation in my gut as we drew closer. We were a few feet away, about to pass them on our route to the dining hall, when Tattoo Guy glanced in our direction. I thought he was just looking away from Ivy, but when he saw me, he simply stared. Stared as if he knew and hated me. As if he could tear me to shreds with that one glance.

Stop it, I told myself. *You're just being paranoid because of everything that's going on. He's clearly arguing with Ivy and you just happened to be in his line of sight.*

Ivy touched his arm, drawing his attention back to her. She gave me a quick, almost apologetic wave. Lorna and I kept walking, but all the way to the dining hall, my spine felt tingly and cold, like he was still staring at me.

Like at any second he was going to drive a knife into my back.

OUT OF IT

"First order of business," Portia Ahronian said, standing up. Everyone else settled in among the pillows and blankets strewn on the floor of the old Billings Chapel. We'd just finished the oath, and I was more than happy to let her take over. My eyes were dry with exhaustion and my brain was fuzzy and tired, even as my heart continued to race with nervousness. "Is anyone going to this lame V-Day dance?"

"You make it sound so attractive," Tiffany joked, reaching for the package of chocolates at the center of the circle. Portia sat down next to Tiffany, her signature gold necklaces glinting in the candlelight, and snagged the chocolate right out of Tiff's hands. Tiff sighed indulgently and chose another piece.

"I thought Billings Girls don't do school dances unless they're mandatory," Ivy put in. There was a touch of disdain in her voice. Before she became one herself, Ivy had never been a big fan of the Billings Girls and their ways.

"We don't. Usually," Rose Sakowitz said. She took a sip of sparkling cider, which we'd decided to bring in lieu of champagne to prevent Vienna from showing up to any more classes hungover. "But I want to see Damon on Valentine's Day and he wants to come to the dance, so . . ."

Rose's on-again-off-again boyfriend, Damon Hazelton, attended The Barton School, another private school nearby.

"Really? You're going?" Amberly asked, wrinkling her pert little nose. Her blond hair was back in a tight bun, and her pink turtleneck sweater made her look like a prima ballerina.

"Maybe we should all think about going," Lorna said, pulling her wide-weave wool sweater tighter around herself as a cold wind whipped through one of the broken stained-glass windows. "I mean . . . it could be fun . . . if we all go."

Kiki and Astrid exchanged a look and rolled their eyes.

"What do you think, Reed?" Lorna asked.

Everyone turned to me expectantly. Once again I felt the weight of responsibility, of my position as leader of the BLS, pressing down on me.

"Yeah. You're strangely silent tonight," Ivy said, sitting up straight and dusting off her hands. Guess we hadn't gotten the floors completely clean on our recent work night.

"Sorry," I said. "I'm just tired." I took a deep breath and let it out slowly. "I think we should go."

"You *do*?" Vienna blurted. "No way."

"Did you guys know that Constance and London are planning the dance?" I asked.

Dumbfounded stares greeted my question. Guess that would be a "no."

"Oh, please. No way," Vienna said, flipping her thick hair over her shoulder. "First of all, London would never participate in something so pedestrian. And secondly, if she did, she would tell me about it."

"Apparently not," I said, not wanting to hurt her feelings, but seeing that it was inevitable. "I saw Constance's planning notebook and asked her about it. She said she and London are doing it together."

There was some uncomfortable shifting in place as everyone eyed Vienna, waiting for her reaction. She and London had been inseparable until the whole BLS thing.

"Oh. Okay," Vienna said, her tone detached as she stared at the floor. "That's that, then."

She reached for the bottle of sparkling cider and brought it to her lips, kicking her head back to down half the contents as if she were trying to drown her sorrows in the nonalcoholic drink. Then she dragged the back of her hand across her lips, smearing her dark red lipstick.

"I'm with Reed and Lorna. I say we go," she said. "We should support our friends."

"But they're not our friends anymore . . . right?" Amberly said, biting her bottom lip.

I was appeased when half a dozen pillows flew at her head.

"Okay! Okay! I'll go!" she said, lifting her arms up to shield her face.

"Right. Now on to the more important question," Tiffany said, yanking a stack of glossy magazines out from her messenger bag and tossing them on the floor with a *thwap*. "What's everyone going to wear?"

There were a few squeals as Lorna and Amberly lunged for the magazines. The girls fell into a babble of giggling, catcalling, and oohing and ahhing. As the circle grew tighter, the better for everyone to share the magazines, I stayed right where I was, on the outskirts, staring toward the rafters of the airy, old chapel.

Noelle should have been there. Of course, if she was, she probably would have rallied against going to some lame Easton event. But still. Who cared? She should have been there.

The longer I stared up at the exposed beams of the high ceiling, the more the voices and laughter of my friends faded into the background. Suddenly, I started to feel as if I was sinking. Into the floor and out of reach. The ceiling loomed farther and farther into the distance, and the blankets sunk with me, smothering me, closing out all light, all happiness, all possibility.

Noelle could die and it would be my fault. Another life lost because I was too inept to help. Too stupid to figure out what was going on around me.

I couldn't do this on my own. I just couldn't. I had to tell someone. But who? Who could possibly know how to handle this?

An image of my father flashed through my mind, and suddenly, I found myself able to breathe again. My dad was the most level-headed person I knew. And he loved me unconditionally. Plus, he was nowhere near Easton, had nothing to do with the community, was in touch with no one at the school. I could tell him without the kidnappers knowing, right? I could tell him and he would tell me what to do.

That was it. I was going to call him right after this meeting. As soon as I got back to Pemberly. I'd use the old pay phone in the hallway just in case these crazy, spying kidnappers could somehow trace my phone. Everything was going to be fine.

"Are you okay?" Ivy said in my ear.

I flinched, sucked out of my brainstorming spiral and back into the now.

"Uh, yeah. Why?" I asked. She sat down right next to me and tucked her phone back into her bag.

"You just seem *really* out of it," Ivy said.

"I told you. I'm just tired," I said, which was part of the truth anyway. "Actually, I should probably head out soon. I haven't even started my English project and after tomorrow I'm going to have an extra-credit assignment from Barber to deal with too."

I pushed myself up to my knees and manically gathered my things, suddenly intent on my new plan. All I could think about was getting back to Pemberly and calling my dad. The thought of that creaky old phone was like a beacon, a big pool of water to a dying man in the desert.

As I reached for my cell to tuck it away, it let out a beep, indicating I had a text.

"Must be from Josh, since everyone else you know is here," Ivy

joked. "Oh, unless it's from Noelle," she added, raising an eyebrow.

If only.

I swallowed hard as I picked up the phone. The text was not from Josh
or Noelle. It was the kidnappers, contacting me with my new directive.

ASSIGNMENT NUMBER TWO: STEAL SOMETHING FABULOUSLY
EXTRAVAGANT FROM A SHOP IN EASTON; THEN MAKE SURE TO
WEAR IT AROUND CAMPUS FOR ALL TO SEE. GET CAUGHT AND
NOELLE DIES. TELL ANYONE ABOUT THIS TEXT AND SHE DIES.

My heart sunk into my toes. They really had to remind me about
that whole silence or death thing didn't they? Looked like I wouldn't
be calling my father after all. I dropped my things back down on the
floor, and sat down cross-legged next to Ivy.

"Changed your mind about your homework, huh?" Ivy said with a
wry smile.

"It can wait," I said. "Pass the chocolate."

If I was really going to steal something tomorrow, I may as well live
it up now. Because considering the fact that I'd never even attempted
to shoplift so much as a ChapStick in my life, there was a very good
chance I was going to get caught. Which meant I'd be spending tomorrow night in jail.

And I had a feeling they didn't serve chocolate and sparkling cider
in jail.

KEEPING SANE

I lay in bed that night, so tired I could feel my skin tightening on my face, feel the weight of my bones as my body pressed into the bed, but still, somehow, unable to sleep. I'd taken a shower upon returning from the chapel, even though it was after eleven. I'd scrubbed my face, washed my hair and blown it dry, brushed my teeth for a good five minutes—all to get my mind to realize that it was time to relax. Time to sleep. Then I'd donned my most comfy flannel pj's, the white-and-purple polka dotted ones my dad had given me for Christmas, and crawled under the covers. Taking a deep breath, I had closed my eyes, and repeated one word to myself slowly, over and over and over again.

Sleep, sleep, sleep, sleep, sleep, sleep, sleep.

And now here I was, an hour later, counting the cracks in my ceiling.

There were more than forty of them. Far too many to be safe. I was going to have to talk to housing about this tomorrow. Or that's what I would have done, if I didn't have to get a pass off campus, go into Easton, and commit petty theft. If life had been at all normal.

With a frustrated groan, I rolled onto my side and fished my phone out of my book bag, which hung from the back of my desk chair. I don't know what I was hoping for. Some message that said, "Psych! We were just kidding! Your next assignment is to eat ten pancakes at breakfast!" No such luck. There were a bunch of new e-mails, but they were all crap from teachers and friends and Scott. Plus one of those stupid mother-daughter love poems my mom had started sending me lately.

Out of nowhere, a tear ran down my cheek. I felt like I was failing, but why? I'd already completed one task. I just had to figure out a way to complete the next. And the one after that. And the one after that. I'd never failed at something like this before—not when I'd been put through all those stupid tests to prove that I was worthy of getting into Billings, not when I'd had to scrounge for my own survival for days on a deserted island. What made me feel so desperate now? I lay flat on my back again, and suddenly tears began streaming from the corners of my eyes. They slid across my temples and wet my hair. My chest heaved with quiet sobs.

Were they watching me right now like they seemed to be at every other moment? Could they somehow see me breaking down? Were they out somewhere, just laughing at me? Laughing at what I'd become at their hands?

I was so tired. So very, very tired. Why couldn't I just sleep? I knew I could think more clearly and handle all of this more soundly if I could just sleep.

Suddenly there was a light knock on the door. I sat up straight and wiped my face with both palms. The door opened before I could even move, and Josh slid into the room.

"Hey," he whispered.

"Hey," I croaked.

Without another word, he shed his coat and kicked off his shoes. Then he crawled into bed with me, wrapping his arms around me and nudging me back down. He nuzzled against me from behind, pressing his ice-cold nose into my neck. He kissed me once, and then he just held me, his breath a perfect rhythm against my skin.

Slowly, I felt myself start to relax. Felt my muscles loosen. Felt my heart unclench. Felt my eyes flutter closed. Thank God for Josh. There was no way I would still be sane without him.

I let out a breath, cuddled deeper into his arms, and promptly, finally, fell asleep.

As I walked up Main Street in Easton on Tuesday, my heart pounded harder than I would have thought possible. I swallowed hard when I saw the small pink-and-white placard hanging above the door of Sweet Nothings, one of the Billings Girls' favorite boutiques. Kiran had shoplifted a few things from this place last year, out of sheer boredom rather than necessity, and she'd never gotten caught once. If I was going to get away with this, Sweet Nothings was the place to be. All I had to do was walk inside, slip something into my pocket and walk out again. I had even dressed up like a person who could actually afford to buy something in the town's most expensive boutique, figuring it would help me feel more comfortable and less conspicuous. I wore the cashmere Dior sweater Kiran had given me last year, and my one pair of diamond earrings, a gift from Walt Whittaker before he had become Constance's one and only. It was the perfect "I've got cash to burn" costume.

I could do this. I could.

I walked right up to the door of Sweet Nothings . . . and then turned around and kept walking.

As I hustled by, I caught the shop owner's quizzical eye through the plate-glass window. I ducked my head guiltily. Dammit. Damn. It. Could I have done anything more conspicuous? What the hell was wrong with me? I hadn't even entered the store yet and already I was on her radar. I yanked my phone out of my bag and pretended to answer it, pausing in full view of the shop owner.

There. See? I just stopped because I was getting a call and I didn't want to be one of those annoying people who have loud cell phone conversations in the middle of a tiny, exclusive shop. I just wanted to avoid irritating your upscale clientele. You should *give* me something for free just for being so damn considerate.

I turned my back to the window and breathed. Let her think I was gabbing away. I should have been sequestered in the library, working on the extra-credit project Mr. Barber had assigned me to make up for my D—yes, D—on yesterday's test. I should have been stressed about my grades right now, not about fulfilling the sadistic requirements of the psycho who had kidnapped my best friend. But there was nothing I could do about it. This was my life. This was what I had to do. Noelle's future depended on it.

"Okay. Right. Bye!" I said loudly into the phone. Then I pantomimed turning it off and shoved it back in my bag.

I am Angelina Jolie in Mr. & Mrs. Smith, I told myself as I walked inside. *I am Sarah the superspy chick from* Chuck. *I am cool and gorgeous and wealthy and can get away with anything.*

"Hey, Reed!"

My hand shot up to cover my heart. Ivy stood near the back of the shop, holding a red silk nightgown. Her dark hair was down around the shoulders of her white coat, and a rust-colored Birkin bag dangled from her forearm. *She* looked like she belonged in here.

But then . . . why *was* she here? She hadn't mentioned anything about going shopping this afternoon. Wouldn't a normal good friend have invited her good friend along?

Not that I'd invited her, but I had a reason. I was here to steal something.

The question was, did she already know that was why I was here? All the little hairs on the back of my neck stood on end as we faced off. Ivy couldn't have something to do with this. Could she?

All of these thoughts passed through my mind in the space of about ten seconds. Ten heady seconds that left me feeling off kilter and completely played.

"What're you doing here?" she asked, placing the hanger back on the rack. "Shopping for a hot date with my ex?"

I gulped against my dry throat. I wished she would stop bringing up Josh so often. As if I wasn't tense enough already. But then, if her mission was to torture me . . .

My eyes darted to the woman behind the counter. She looked down her aquiline nose at me and sniffed, although her forehead was so overly botoxed her expression didn't change one bit. Then she got back to hand-pricing a stack of cashmere sweaters piled up on the counter, her short, dark hair falling forward over her sharp cheekbones.

Ivy's brow knit as she approached me. "I'm just kidding. You know

I'm happy for you guys." She nudged me with her shoulder. "God, you've been so serious lately. Is everything okay?"

Her eyes were warm and concerned and just like that, my suspicions died away, replaced by an overwhelming sense of guilt. Not every one of my friends was a psycho. Statistically speaking, I'd probably never have another psycho friend as long as I lived. Ariana and Sabine had already cornered the market.

"Yeah. Everything's fine," I replied, moving past her and pretending to browse. I fingered a silky, green-and-white scarf and checked the price tag. Fifty bucks. Probably not "fabulously extravagant" enough to impress the kidnappers. "I'm just looking for a birthday present for my mom," I lied, moving on to a rack of winter hats. It was the same story I'd given Double H's secretary to get my pass off campus. Her birthday *was* actually coming up, so if the woman cared to check my story it would have added up.

"Oh, cool," Ivy said. She walked back over to the lingerie rack, picked up the nightgown again, and smiled at me. "On second thought," she said. "This is totally mine."

She sidled around a cascading rack of cocktail dresses and headed for the counter. Even in all my conspicuousness and on-the-verge-of-peeing-in-my-pants tension, I couldn't help wondering who she planned on wearing that nightgown for. Tattoo Guy? I watched from the corner of my eye as the shop owner slid the sweaters aside so she could ring up Ivy's purchase and decided now was not the time to ponder Ivy's love life. For the moment, the woman was distracted. This was my chance.

I turned around and found myself in the back alcove where the shoes were displayed. That was never going to work. I couldn't exactly hide a pair of Uggs in my pockets. I heard the crinkle of tissue paper as the proprietor folded and wrapped Ivy's nightgown. There was still time. I strode to the other side of the store where sunglasses and flip-flops and bathing suits dangled from silver hooks—everything the rich denizens of Easton might need for their winter getaways. I couldn't exactly sport a bikini to class tomorrow, but sunglasses . . . those were a possibility.

I reached for a pair of Gucci's with the logo imprinted all along the sides. The tag read $350. I held my breath. Just slip them from the rack and into your pocket. One swift motion. My heart throbbed in my ears and my eyes stung. I couldn't believe I was doing this. Could not believe it.

But Kiran would have gotten away with ten pairs by now.

Do it, Reed! I heard her say in my ear. *Do it! Do it now!*

I was just slipping the glasses from the metal rack when Ivy came up behind me.

"Wow! Nice gift!" she said loudly.

I dropped my hand so fast it slammed into the rack and half a dozen pair of two-hundred-dollar-and-up sunglasses clattered to the floor. The woman behind the counter *tsk*ed under her breath, dropped her pen, and walked around to clean up the mess.

"I'm really sorry," I stammered, backing up. My skin was so hot I was sure I was about to melt into a puddle on the floor. "I didn't mean to—"

"It's fine, dear," she said, her words placating, but her tone unkind. "Happens all the time."

I whipped around to face Ivy, sweat pricking the back of my neck. "You know what? I could really go for some coffee. Want to hit Starbucks?"

"Sure," she said, lifting a shoulder. "Oh, but I actually have to get some cash."

"Perfect!" I blurted.

"What?" she asked, completely baffled.

"You go hit the ATM and I'll meet you there!" I said, my eyes wide. I sounded manic even to my own ears. "I'm just gonna look at a few more things."

"Ooookay," Ivy said, eyeing me skeptically. "But are you sure you want coffee? You're kinda hyper already."

The shop owner, still crouched on the floor, tried to hide a laugh.

"I'm sure. I'll be there in five," I said.

As Ivy left the shop, the little bell above the door tinkling behind her, I turned around and desperately surveyed the area. Chunky sweaters, distressed jeans, and faux-fur-collared coats stared back at me. Tears stung my eyes. Who was I kidding? I couldn't do this. This was not me. I realized with a sudden sinking dread that I had failed. That the kidnapper had hit on the one thing I was not capable of doing.

But Noelle needed me. It was this one little infraction—this one middle-school dare—or her life. What the hell was wrong with me? Why couldn't I just do it?

The store owner stood up and smoothed her black skirt. "Can I help you find anything?" she asked, sounding like she'd rather wrestle a pack of hyenas. Her eyes narrowed as she looked me up and down.

She knew. She knew why I was there. What I was trying to do. Of course she did. I was acting so guilty I may as well have had the word scrawled across my forehead in bright red letters.

"I'm good, thanks," I managed to say.

As she went back to the counter, I wandered over to the shoes again, just trying to regain my composure. There was a rack of half-off socks back there, and I grabbed the first pair I saw—thick, black, and gray striped ones, probably meant for cozy nights by the fire at the ski house in Vail. They were only ten bucks. I figured I'd at least buy something to throw the woman off my scent. Prove her suspicions wrong, even though they so weren't.

"Hey, Mom!"

A pretty girl with jet-black curls stepped out of the storeroom at the back of the shoe section and strode right by me, up to the counter. She was about my age, but petite, with a lip piercing and a ton of eye shadow.

"Louise! There you are," the woman said, exasperated. "Your break was over fifteen minutes ago."

"Sorry. I was on the phone with Christine, and you know how she gets," Louise said, rolling her eyes. "Go ahead and grab dinner. I got this."

Louise's mom patted her on the shoulder. "I'll be back in half an hour."

Then she turned and walked toward the back room. As she passed me by, she gave me a long, admonishing look, but kept walking. Behind the counter, Louise popped a pair of ear buds in her ears, yanked a graphic novel out from under the counter, and leaned back against the wall to read.

Well. Things had just turned right around, hadn't they?

Slowly, I walked up to the side of the counter, where a bevy of glittering necklaces were displayed on small, hanging racks. Louise looked up as I approached and gave me a quick smile, then returned to her reading. I lifted the tiny white price tag on the first necklace. It looked like something the new Lorna might wear. A string of delicate, white beads with every tenth bead replaced by a rhinestone-encrusted flower. The price was $250.

I glanced at Louise again. She was engrossed. Carefully, casually, I slid the necklace off the display, folded it around my hand, and then stuffed my hand into one of the thick, woolen socks. My palms were sweating profusely, and for a second the necklace stuck to my skin, but I wiggled my fingers and it fell free, nestled perfectly inside the pocket of wool.

"I'll take these," I said, dropping the socks on the counter.

Louise pulled one ear bud from her ear and glanced at the price tag. She keyed the numbers into the register and snapped her gum.

"That'll be ten sixty," she said.

I dove into my bag and fumbled out my wallet. She waited patiently while I extracted a ten and a single and shakily handed over the bills.

"You need a bag?" she asked, jamming down on a button. The cash register slid open with a clang.

"No!" I practically shouted. I plucked the socks off the counter and into my handbag, shoving them as far down as they would go. Louise looked at me like I'd just escaped from a mental asylum.

"Okay. You don't *have* to take one," she said a bit sarcastically.

I laughed. "Sorry. Too many Red Bulls today."

She grinned and rolled her eyes. "I hear ya," she said, sliding my forty cents across the counter. "Have a good one!"

Then she popped her ear bud back into her ear and picked up her book. That was it. Easy peasy. Like ripping off a Band-Aid. I grabbed my change, turned around, and made for the front of the store like I was running for the carousel at the state fair when I was a little kid. Pure and utter joy coursed through my veins. Not to mention this kind of euphoric, all-powerful feeling. I'd gotten away with it. I'd actually gotten away with it.

"Hey! Wait!" Louise shouted.

I froze with my hand on the door. My heart choked off all air supply. Across the street I could see Ivy sitting in the front window at Starbucks, sipping a coffee, waiting for me. Little did she know that if she was ever going to see me again, she was going to have to bail me out at the Easton police station.

I turned around to face my accuser.

"Here!" Louise said. "You forgot your receipt!"

She held out a tiny white scrap of paper.

"My mom freaks if I forget to give them out. There's a special discount coupon at the bottom and she thinks it's the holy grail of repeat business," Louise said, shaking the receipt like she was offering a bone to a dog.

My brain was taking way too long to catch up. Somehow I managed to reach out and take the receipt, but my expression was completely confused.

"Mothers, huh?" I heard myself say.

"Can't live with them, but they do pay for the pizza," Louise joked back. "See ya."

She sashayed back behind the counter and I turned around and shoved open the door. A gush of cold air hit me in the face, waking me from my stupor, and just like that, I was free. I crumpled the receipt and tossed it into a garbage can as I crossed the street to meet my friend.

Discount coupon or no discount coupon, there was no way I was ever stepping foot in that store again.

JEWELS

I had committed a crime. I was a felon. A thief. Every time I looked down at the long, beaded necklace, dangling low on my chest, my stomach twisted. I couldn't believe I'd actually felt proud of myself for even a moment. What had I accomplished, really? I'd managed to hide something from a girl who probably wouldn't have noticed if a nuclear bomb had gone off under the countertop. And I'd probably gotten her in trouble. Once her mom realized a $250 necklace had gone missing on her watch, Louise was dead. That woman had no-nonsense written all over her. Would she fire Louise? Take away her iPod? Stop buying her the pizza she so clearly lived for?

I was an awful human being.

"Hey. Great necklace!" Diana Waters said to me as we slid our trays down the food line at dinner that night. Diana was one of my few friends outside the Billings circle. With her athletic, tomboy style, jewelry wasn't something I ever would have thought she'd notice. But of course she noticed my one stolen item. "Where'd you get it?"

"I . . . it . . . was a gift," I lied. My heart pounded in my ears. Was that cafeteria lady with the ladle staring at me? Did she know something?

Looking away, I grabbed a big bowl of mashed potatoes and added it to my tray, which was already loaded down with marinara-sauce-covered spaghetti and garlic bread. Comfort food at its finest.

"WTF, Reed? Are you carbo-loading for some marathon I don't know about?" Portia asked, glancing over her shoulder at me. Her tray held only a small salad, a bottle of water, and a plain piece of grilled chicken. All the better to fit into that size oo houndstooth Chanel skirt she was sporting.

"Sorry if it's not my goal to disappear when I turn sideways," I replied.

Portia smirked. Clearly, she was proud of the fact that she had wrists so skinny she could practically wrap her fingers around them twice.

"See you in class, D," I said to Diana.

She gave me a wave, still eyeing the necklace admiringly. Part of me wanted to just tear it off and give it to her, but my instructions were clear. I had to be seen wearing my stolen item on campus. So I grabbed a Sprite and fell into step with Portia, lifting my chin high to ensure the necklace was on full display as we walked into the dining hall. Already the tables were jam-packed with students, noshing, talking, laughing, and even—in the case of one of the guys' tables—

pinging grapes off one another's heads. Portia turned toward the tables at the center of the room where the rest of the Billings Literary Society members sat, but I paused when I saw Josh waving me down from the far side of the room.

"I'll catch up," I told her.

She rolled her eyes slightly. "Ah, young love."

I rolled my eyes back. Maybe that was Portia's problem. Maybe that was why she didn't want to go to the Sweethearts Dance. She hadn't had a boyfriend since I'd known her. In lighter times, I would have immediately focused on finding her one to curb her acerbic tendencies and make Valentine's Day fun for her, but I kind of had a lot on my plate right then.

"Hey," I said, hovering at the end of Josh's lonely table.

He used his toe to nudge the chair across from him out from under the table. "Saved you a seat," he said with a grin.

There was nothing I would have liked better than to sink into that chair and hang out with him for the next hour, but I'd been kind of neglecting the BLS girls lately. Besides, if anyone was going to actually notice the illegal bling around my neck, it was my girlfriends. And the more people who noticed it, the better. Somehow it had to get back to this mysterious kidnapper that I was sporting my stolen goods.

"Actually, I promised the girls I'd sit with them tonight," I said, biting my lip. "But maybe I'll come over and join you for dessert?"

Josh's face fell. He glanced past me at the Billings table and I saw his jaw clench and unclench. There wasn't much in this world Josh hated more than he hated the Billings Girls. He thought they were shallow, obnoxious, and self-serving, and even though I knew them better than he did, I'd never been able to convince him otherwise. As a result, my friends had always been a bit of a thorn in the side of our relationship.

"Fine. Yeah. Whatever," he said.

"Don't be mad," I implored. "I promise I'll come over later."

Josh forced a smile. "I'm cool. I've got some reading to catch up on anyway."

"Thanks."

I walked over to my usual table and sat down in the last chair, next to Portia, trying not to dwell on the fact that Josh was clearly pissed. Tiffany was sitting across from Portia, her short, dark curls pushed back from her forehead by a dark red headband. She was scrolling through pictures on her digital camera with Rose hanging over her shoulder to better see the frames.

"Hey, ladies," I said, trying for a light tone. "What're you looking at?"

"Shots from St. Barths," Tiffany replied.

Rose laughed at something on the screen, her red curls shaking. "Check out this one of you and Noelle."

She turned the camera around so I could see. There, on the screen, were me and Noelle, clad in bathing suits, our arms looped around each other as we model-posed for the camera. Noelle's lips were pursed and my tongue touched my top lip, in what I thought at the time was a sexy pose. Now it just looked ridiculous. As my friends laughed and teased me, a bubble choked my throat.

I reached down and fiddled with my necklace.

Noelle. Where are you?

"Hey," Ivy said, dropping down across from me. She put her tray down and her eyes instantly went to my necklace. Not surprising, considering I was now twisting it tightly around my pinky. "Wow. Reed, that's beautiful," she said, reaching out to finger the beads. I let it uncurl and it lengthened out again. "Did you get that at Sweet Nothings this afternoon?"

"Um, yeah," I said, struggling to speak past the throat bubble.

"It's so pretty. Why didn't you show it to me at Starbucks?" Ivy asked, lifting the strap of her book bag over her head and turning to hang it on the back of her chair.

"Yeah and why did you just tell that Diana person it was a gift?" Portia asked, arching one eyebrow.

I swallowed hard as my heart clenched. Rose, Tiffany, Portia, and Ivy all stared at me, clearly intrigued. They knew. Of course they knew. My friends were intimately aware of the shortcomings of my bank account. We all knew I couldn't have afforded such a thing. Maybe I should just admit it. Tell them I'd gone over to the dark side—that I'd shoplifted. They all knew that Kiran had done it a few times. It wasn't *so* scandalous. But the fact that I was poor would probably make the act seem pathetic rather than daring. And the very idea of seeming pathetic to them made my stomach coil.

Which meant it was time to start spewing more lies.

"I . . . yeah . . . I didn't want to tell her where I got it," I said, trying as hard as I could to sound casual. I reached for my Sprite and took a sip. "You know. 'Cause then she would go buy one and then someone else would want one. . . ."

"God, don't you hate that?" Portia said, spearing a cucumber with her fork. "When you get something you like and then suddenly *everyone* has one?"

"Yeah. Totally," I said, my heart unclenching slightly.

"I think I saw those. Up on the counter, right?" Ivy said, narrowing her eyes. "They were, like, three hundred dollars."

"Whoa. That's some major coin for fake jewels," Tiffany said.

"Since when does scholarship girl have cash like that lying around?" Portia asked.

"I . . . I just . . . had some Christmas money, still," I said. The beads suddenly felt sharp around my neck, and my skin started to itch. I pushed my chair back from the table. "I gotta go. I'll . . . be right back."

I turned around and fled the room, my vision blurred by hot tears of mortification. I could feel everyone in the dining hall staring at me, talking about me, whispering and laughing. This wasn't a new sensation for me, of course, but there was no getting used to it. No matter how many times I was the subject of gossip or the butt of jokes, it never got any easier. Out in the marble-floored foyer, I shoved my way into the bathroom and leaned over the first porcelain sink, heaving for breath.

I couldn't stand lying in general. Lying about the fact that I'd stolen something was even worse. My skin burned and I pressed my palms against the counter, leaning farther over the sink.

"It's for Noelle," I whispered to myself. "Just chill the freak out before someone starts suspecting something."

Taking a deep breath, I turned on the cold water and splashed my face a few times. When I looked up at my reflection, dark mascara ran down my cheeks. I grabbed a paper towel and dabbed off the mess. The delicate skin under my eyes screamed in protest against the harsh paper, and when I looked at myself again, the area was red and raw. I took a few more deep breaths for good measure and waited for my skin to cool off.

It's going to be fine, I thought. *It's all going to be fine.*

The problem was, I didn't believe it. But I had to at least pretend that I did. I rolled my shoulders back, turned, and yanked open the door. In the foyer I nearly ran right into Sawyer Hathaway.

"Whoa! Hey!" he said, grabbing on to my shoulders in an attempt to steady us both. "Oh," he said, his face falling when he saw it was me.

"Sorry," I said, ducking my head and trying to get around him.

"Wait. Reed."

I stopped and turned to face him, but found myself unable to look him in the eye.

"I don't want to do this," he said. He had his hands in the pockets of his wool coat, as if he'd just come in from the outside. He gestured with them as he spoke, opening the sides to reveal the striped lining.

"Do what?" I asked.

"That thing, you know, where I don't talk to you because of . . . you know . . . what happened with . . . us. Not that we were even an 'us' . . . ," he said. Then he bit off an embarrassed laugh. "Whatever. I don't want to be that guy."

I looked up at him then, hope tickling my insides. His blond hair was pushed back from his face, and his blue eyes somehow looked bluer, darker, than usual.

"Why be a cliche?" I joked.

He cracked a smile. "Exactly."

I smiled back. Then we both looked at the floor.

"I'm not saying it doesn't suck," he told me. "Seeing you with Upton and now Josh. I mean, I've heard you've got a history with that guy, but after what he did to Jen—"

"He didn't do anything to Jen," I said defensively. "They just broke up. And it was, like, two years ago."

Sawyer nodded. "I know. I just . . . I guess I'm overly suspicious of anyone who broke her heart, you know? Especially now that she's . . ."

He paused and shook his head. "Anyway . . ." He looked at me suddenly, as if he had just really looked at me for the first time, and his forehead creased with concern. "Hey," he said, taking a step closer to me. "Are you okay?"

I blinked, surprised that he cared enough to ask. I felt so alone I think I would have been surprised by kindness from anyone at that moment. But from Sawyer, it was particularly touching. My eyes smarted all over again. "I thought you were going to hate me forever," I said.

Sawyer sighed. "I never *hated* you. Yeah, I wanted to . . . to be . . ." He trailed off and looked away. Both of us blushed. "But I'm over it."

"Yeah?" I asked.

"Over it enough to give a crap when you look like that," he said lightly.

"Thanks a lot," I joked halfheartedly. But the tears were now brimming in my eyes. God, I was getting sick of crying. Why could I not stop myself from crying?

"Reed," Sawyer said, reaching for me. "Come on. Whatever it is, it's gonna be okay."

Then he tugged me to him and we hugged. It was a totally platonic, friendly hug. And basically, exactly what I needed at that moment. I managed not to burst out into full-on tears, but instead sniffled, blinked them back, and breathed. I just breathed. And it felt good.

"Thanks," I said, pulling away.

Sawyer smiled. "Anytime."

Then he looked past me and his skin paled. "Oh. Hey, man."

My stomach sunk. I turned around and there was Josh. He'd just stepped out of the dining hall, without his stuff, obviously coming after me.

"Um, hey," he said. His eyes darted between me and Sawyer and his jaw suddenly set. "Well. I guess you don't need me, then."

He turned on his heel and fled back into the dining hall.

"Josh!"

I went after him, casting an apologetic look over my shoulder at Sawyer, hoping he'd understand. But by the time I'd opened the door, Josh had grabbed his things and was halfway across the room, headed for the outside door, which he let slam loudly, pointedly, behind him.

Suddenly, my cell phone beeped in my pocket, and I quickly fumbled for it. I'd just received a new text.

ASSIGNMENT NUMBER TWO COMPLETE. ANOTHER JOB WELL-DONE. YOUR NEW INSTRUCTIONS WILL ARRIVE SHORTLY.

My eyes darted to Ivy at the end of my table. She was lifting a forkful of rice to her mouth, listening intently to something Portia was saying, but her left hand was hidden under the table. Across the room, Headmaster Hathaway tilted his ear toward Mr. Owens, but his eyes were on me. Then Gage and Graham walked across my line of vision. They looked at me, then Gage whispered something. They both laughed. At their table, Constance, London, and Missy were all huddled in conversation, looking at something flat on the center of the table. Was it a phone? Had they just sent the text? Suddenly, a door slammed behind me and I whirled around. No one was there. I couldn't even tell which of the two doors had closed. At that moment, my phone beeped again. My hand was shaking so hard I could barely hit the button to open it. When I finally did, the text made my blood run cold.

NICE NECKLACE, BY THE WAY.

PROOF

That night I sat at my desk, my laptop screen glowing in front of me, working on my paper for English class. At least, that's what anyone who had walked into the room would have thought I was doing, what with all the books on Jane Austen's life open around my laptop, and the title "A Day in the Life of Jane Austen" typed across the top of my Word document along with my name and the date. Really I was staring out the window at the stars, contemplating how completely screwed up my life was.

Noelle had been kidnapped and I was the only one who could save her. I was lying to my best friends about where she was and lying to the headmaster about her excuse for missing classes, which basically meant I was aiding and abetting the kidnappers because, thanks to me, no one even knew the girl was missing. Oh, and I had committed petty theft. At least I thought it was petty. At what price range did it stop being petty and start being grand? The very idea that I had to even ponder a question like that made me sick to my stomach. It made me wonder who the hell I had become.

Meanwhile, Josh, the one person who had always been there for me, and who was currently my rock in seriously choppy waters, had caught me getting intimate with not one, but two guys in four days.

I bet Jane Austen never had to deal with crap like this.

Suddenly, my phone beeped. My heart lurched into my throat. On the desk, my iPhone lit up with a new text. My fingers trembled as I reached for it. It read simply:

ASSIGNMENT NUMBER THREE: PISS OFF THE HEADMASTER.

I groaned and dropped the phone down again, beyond disgusted. I pressed my elbows into the open books on either side of my keyboard, and hung my head in my hands.

Piss off the headmaster? Steal something from Easton? What the hell did these tasks have to do with saving Noelle's life? These kidnappers were insanely juvenile. I mean, didn't they know they'd snatched one of the wealthiest teenagers in the country? Shouldn't they have been, I don't know, calling up Mr. Lange and demanding five million dollars in unmarked bills rather than leading me through a series of playground pranks?

Was I really going to let them do this to me?

No.

Surprised by a sudden surge of anger, I grabbed my phone, and hit reply. Standing up, I paced across my room as I texted back.

My fingers were still trembling, but this time they were trembling with ire.

IF U WANT ME TO KEEP DOING THIS STUPID CRAP U NEED TO SEND ME PROOF THAT NOELLE IS ALIVE AND OK. NOW!!!!!

I hit send, held my breath, and waited. I paced to the door, pressed my forehead against the cool glass of my full-length mirror, and breathed, making a steam cloud just under my nose. I counted to ten before looking down at the phone. Nothing. I paced over to the slim window looking out over the quad, pressed my forehead against that freezing cold glass and breathed another cloud. Once more, I counted to ten. Still nothing. I was just about to turn around and pace back, when my laptop pinged, indicating I had an e-mail.

I walked back over to my desk, my heart pounding in my ears, and brought up Internet Explorer. The message was from someone apparently named x7hrp8q. There was no subject, but there was an attachment.

Suddenly, I couldn't breathe. I reached for the mouse pad, and clicked open the attachment. It was a video. At first, static filled the screen, but then, there she was. Noelle. The video was grainy, but it was her. She was tied to a metal chair, her hands behind her back. The chair sat in the center of a gray-walled room, with no other furniture in sight, and there was a fresh gash across her cheek. I gasped out loud and stepped back, my hand over my mouth.

"Reed," Noelle said to the camera, her eyes wide. She glanced over her shoulder and leaned closer. As close as she could with her arms straining behind her. Her hair stuck to the drying blood on her cheek and there was something wild about the look in her eyes. Something I'd never seen before. "Whatever they're telling you to do, just do it!" she hissed. "Please!"

And then, with a buzz, the video went black.

"Omigod," I whispered, sitting down on my bed and curling my knees up under my chin. "Omigod, omigod, omigod."

I hadn't even begun to contemplate what it might all mean when there was a sudden peal of laughter in the next room. My head popped up and I turned to look at the wall, as if I could see through to the other side.

That was Ivy. My friend. My confidant.

My best friend's worst enemy. The ex of my current boyfriend.

Had my suspicions in Sweet Nothings been correct? Was there a reason Ivy had cracked up laughing two seconds after the video feed had gone blank?

Suddenly, my meager dinner revolted on me. Sweat bursting out along my hairline, I turned and sprinted through the door and into the bathroom. I just made it to the first stall before throwing up. When I was done, I flushed, sat back on the cold tile floor, and wiped my lips with a huge wad of toilet paper. I hung my head in my hands, heaving for breath, picturing Ivy alone in her room, laughing at me.

Was it possible, really possible, that I was being betrayed, played, and tortured by yet another "friend"?

When I really started to think about it, I realized that there are many, many ways to piss off a headmaster. From the mundane, like letting out a string of curses right in front of him, to the profane, like streaking across campus, to the blasphemous, like destroying some important historical Easton artifact. But I had a hunch that the cursing wouldn't be big enough, that streaking might send me to the nurse with frostbite, and the destruction would be a tad redundant, seeing as I'd already been blamed (along with my friends) for the torching of Gwendolyn Hall.

So as Josh and I made our way from breakfast over to the chapel for morning services on Wednesday, I made my final decision. I would go with a fourth option: the ridiculous. I just hoped that in the next five minutes I could get up the guts to do it.

"I can't believe they actually sent you a video of her," Josh whispered, his hands in the pockets of his coat. His shoulder bumped mine every so often as we walked, keeping us close together without having to expose our already cold-chapped fingers to the elements. "You really couldn't tell where she was?"

I shook my head, blinking as a sharp wind stung my eyes. Neither one of us had mentioned the incident with Sawyer, and I was kind of hoping it wouldn't come up. That maybe Josh had thought about it and realized it was perfectly innocent and that his storming away had been an overreaction. I had to hope, because it wasn't something I was capable of dealing with right now.

"The whole thing was about eight seconds long," I replied. "And there was literally nothing in the background."

Josh cursed under his breath. He sidestepped and ducked as Gage and a couple of the other guys went tearing by, tossing snow at one another. They weren't even industrious enough to make snowballs. They were just grabbing up snow and flinging it.

"Who the hell is doing this?" Josh said through his teeth.

I swallowed hard, the lump that masqueraded as my heart these days felt dead and lifeless inside my chest.

"I have a feeling I know who it is," I told him, glancing back over my shoulder. Ivy was walking at least twenty yards behind us, huddled together with Vienna, Tiffany, and Rose.

"You do? And you didn't lead with that?" Josh asked, his eyebrows shooting up.

"Honestly, I just . . . don't think you're gonna like it," I told him.

We came to the final bend in the path before reaching the front of the chapel. I tugged him toward a bench to get out of the way of the others, but didn't sit, seeing as the surface was covered in ice and snow.

"Who is it?" he asked, ducking his head toward mine.

I watched over his shoulder until my friends had scurried past. Then I took a deep breath.

"I think it might be Ivy."

Josh stepped back as if he'd been slapped. "What? Are you cracked? Why would Ivy do something like this?"

"Maybe to get back at us?" I said, lifting my shoulders. "I know she talks a big game, but, call me crazy, I don't think she's so psyched about you and me getting back together."

Josh scoffed and reeled away from me like I was so nuts I didn't even merit an argument. With one long stride he was back on the pathway to the chapel and I was jogging to catch up.

"Josh, hear me out!" I said, grabbing his arm. "Ivy has *always* hated Noelle. And lately she's been hanging out with some shady dude who has serial killer written all over him."

"Come on, Reed. Ivy?" Josh whispered angrily. "I think I know her a little better than you do, and I *know* she could never do anything like this."

His comment stung. Did he really need to remind me that he and Ivy had been so very close? Besides, he hadn't seen all the things I'd seen. Like the fact that Ivy had been waiting in Sweet Nothings when I'd gone there to shoplift. Almost as if she *knew* what the assignment was and where I would go. As if she wanted to make sure I would complete it. Plus she was the one who'd made a point of telling everyone how much my new necklace was worth. And hadn't she had her phone out that night in the chapel right before I'd gotten the text with my shoplifting assignment? It all added up.

"Oh, yeah? Well then try explaining to me why, last night, the second that video was done playing on my computer, I heard her laughing in the next room?"

Josh and I both fell silent as Mr. Barber and Mrs. Carr strode by us on their way into the chapel.

"Um, I don't know. People laugh all the time for all kinds of reasons, Reed," Josh said impatiently. "Ever hear of the word 'coincidence'?"

Okay. Now he was being just plain rude.

"There are no coincidences," I said, leveling him with a stare.

For a long moment he was silent, just gazing back into my eyes as if he was waiting for me to reveal the punch line.

"You know what? You need to tell someone about this," he said finally. "An adult. Clearly you should not be dealing with this on your own. You're starting to lose your grip."

He turned abruptly and speed-walked up the steps to the chapel, twisting sideways to get past a couple of sophomore guys hanging out in the doorway.

"I don't get you!" I yelled, chasing after him. "None of us thought Ariana was capable of killing Thomas. And Sabine? She was the nicest person on earth until she pulled a gun on me."

He whirled around and I nearly slammed into his chest. "Yeah, and shot Ivy," he said. "Ivy's a victim, Reed, not a villain."

"Or maybe the fact that she took a bullet because the guy she was dating was trying to save *me* instead of *her* is just one more reason for her to hate us," I hissed, more than a little aware of the fact that dozens of students and teachers were now well within earshot.

Josh's eyes went cold. Dead, almost. He turned around without another word, trudged over to the senior guys' section on the back left side of the chapel, and sat down. As I walked past him toward the junior girls' area, he didn't even glance in my direction. It was official. If he hadn't been pissed off at me after the shirtless Upton incident and the Sawyer hug, he was now.

"Hey, Reed!" Lorna whispered, sliding closer to Kiki so I could sit down at the end of the pew next to her. "What was that all about? Josh does not look happy."

"Trouble in paradise?" Missy Thurber sneered, turning around in her seat to look at us.

"No one was talking to you, Missy," I snapped.

"Wow. You really are the queen bitch these days, aren't you?" she replied before facing forward again.

"Everything's fine with Josh," I told Lorna quietly. "We're just having a slight disagreement about what to do for Valentine's Day."

"Sometimes I think that holiday is more trouble than it's worth," Astrid groused from down the pew.

"Preaching to the choir, sister," I replied.

I took a deep breath and tapped my foot impatiently as everyone around me whispered and did some last-minute cramming for quizzes or texted on their phones. I wished Double H would get this party started already. I was in no mood to sit in this chapel any longer than I had to. For the first time, I wasn't dreading one of the kidnapper's tasks. I was definitely in the mood to blow off some steam.

"Good morning, everyone!" Headmaster Hathaway called out from the podium at the front of the chapel.

Instantly, everyone around me fell silent. My original plan had been to wait until Hathaway had launched into his usual slate of announcements about club meetings and alumni days and keeping the campus clean, but my impatience got the best of me. I jumped up, stepped into the aisle, and screamed at the top of my lungs.

"Snake!" I shouted, pointing at the floor, my eyes wide. "Snake! There's a snake in the chapel!" Every single person in the room turned to gape at me.

"Reed! What're you doing?" Lorna cried.

"There's nothing there," Astrid said.

"Miss Brennan, kindly take your seat," Mr. Hathaway ordered, his words clipped.

"Snake!" I screamed again, edging around my imaginary reptile. My face was so hot I actually thought it might spontaneously burst into flame, but still I pressed on. "Snake! Everyone get out! There's a snake in the chapel!"

"Miss Brennan!" Headmaster Hathaway shouted.

Missy, Constance, and some of the other girls in their row started to laugh. I grabbed Missy by the shoulder and yanked her out of the pew. "Snake! Run, Missy! There's a snake!"

"Get off me, you freak!" she shouted back, tearing my fingers off her shoulder.

"Miss Brennan!" the headmaster roared.

I almost laughed. Guess I had officially succeeded in pissing him off.

Now people were starting to stand up from their seats to better see the nutjob in the aisle. Some of them looked appalled, others amused. Gage stood *on* the pew, laughing a big belly laugh. I saw a few flash-bulbs pop as people whipped out their phones to commemorate the morning that Reed Brennan finally lost her marbles.

I bet a lot of them thought it was a long time coming.

"Snake! Snake!" I screamed.

Sawyer jumped up from his pew and put his hands on my shoulders. "Reed? What are you doing? Are you okay?"

"Snake!" I screamed in his face, feeling awful for pulling him into this. "Snake! Snake! Snake!"

Finally the headmaster gave the nod to the two security guards stationed at the back of the chapel. They both marched forward and each of them grabbed an arm, turning me around, and basically dragging me out the door. Sawyer tripped backward and stood there in the aisle, dumbfounded as he watched us go. I purposely averted my eyes from the area where Josh and his friends sat. I wasn't sure I wanted to see his reaction to all this.

"Snake?" I said mournfully over my shoulder, just for fun. As the guards manhandled me outside and the door was slammed behind us, half the chapel burst into applause and cheers.

Nice. I bet that pissed Double H off more than anything.

Five minutes later I was perched on one of the cots in the nurse's office, the starched, white coverlet crunching beneath me as the nurse tugged the thermometer out of my mouth.

"Normal," Nurse Raine said, appearing surprised. She shrugged and tossed the disposable tip into the garbage. "You sure you're feeling all right, dear?"

"I'm fine," I said dismissively. "I don't even know why I'm here."

The nurse stood up straight and shrugged. I suppose that after a number of years of dealing with kids trying to get out of tests, avoid ex-boyfriends, and spend the day sleeping, she'd pretty much seen it all.

"Here. Drink this and lie down," she said, handing me a paper cup full of water. "I'm sure you'll feel better after a nap."

"Thanks."

As she walked out her hand reached for the light switch, but she paused when she saw Headmaster Hathaway walking in. My heart thumped extra hard in my chest. What was he doing here? And how had he gotten here so fast?

"I'll take it from here, Ms. Raine," he said, tugging his leather gloves from his hands. He slipped off his overcoat, hung it over the back of a chair, and sat, tugging up the legs of his suit pants slightly.

"That must've been a very quick morning service," I joked, trying to mask my nervousness.

"We need to talk, Reed," he said without preamble. He leaned forward, forearms on his thighs, and laced his fingers together. Headmaster Hathaway was actually a nice-looking guy, with his light brown hair, tan skin, and chiseled cheekbones. But there was something about his demeanor that made me want to squirm. He tried to act like he was a friend to the students, but there was always some kind of backhanded threat or ominous warning just waiting on the tip of his tongue. "There's something going on with you, and I need you to tell me what it is."

And just like that, my tongue started to itch. I could tell him. I could just tell him and let him deal with it. He was an adult. A person of authority. He was even friends with Noelle's parents. He'd walk right out of here, call them, and they'd get a SWAT team on Noelle's ass in about fifteen seconds. Josh was right. I didn't have to deal with this on my own. I was, technically, just a kid.

Right as I was about to open my mouth and spill it all, my cell phone let out a loud beep. Instantly all my blood rushed into my face. What was I thinking? I couldn't tell anyone anything. Noelle's life hung in the balance. After everything I'd been through here at Easton, I knew all too well how fragile life was. How easy it was for some people to take it from others. I couldn't risk losing Noelle.

If I lost her, I had no idea what I would do. And besides, I didn't entirely trust Mr. Hathaway. Who knew if he would actually do the right thing?

"I'm fine," I told him, my voice thick. "Really. I just . . . needed to vent."

Headmaster Hathaway blew out a sigh and hung his head. He made a temple of his forefingers and held them over his mouth as he looked up at me again.

"I'm sorry that you choose not to trust me, Reed," he said slowly, his eyes like two rounds of coal. "But if you won't tell me what's going on, I'm just going to have to find out for myself."

"KIDNAPPED"

"Get off your butt, Reed. We're kidnapping you!"

Under the current circumstances, hearing such a thing might have scared me, but it was coming from Tiffany and she had a big, fat smile on her face as she walked into my room. I sat up on my bed, dropping the history book I was trying to concentrate on. My extra-credit assignment was due on Tuesday and I had barely made a dent. Letting my friends kidnap me right now would not be the most responsible choice.

But who could worry about being responsible at a time like this?

"Who's we?" I asked, leaning to the side to try to see around her. Rose waved at me from the doorway.

"Rose and I are taking you to the Botanical for a little Saturday morning R and R," Tiffany said, grabbing me by the wrists and hauling me up. She clapped her hands together. "Let's go. Coat, hat, bag. Go, go, go!"

"Okay, if your intention is to relax me, you're not off to a great start," I said with a laugh.

"She has a point, Tiff," Rose said. "Dial it down a notch."

"Sorry," Tiffany said. "Spa days excite me." She looked me up and down, her brow creased with consternation. "Why are you not moving?"

I glanced at my iPhone, sitting silent and lifeless on my desk. What if the kidnappers texted while I was in the middle of a massage? What if I had to do something on campus right away? Maybe being away from here for too long would be a big mistake.

But then, none of the kidnapper's assignments had been immediate. And besides, it was Valentine's Day, and I hadn't spoken to Josh in almost forty-eight hours. I had no idea if he still intended to take me to the dance tonight as we'd planned, or if he was going to call me and cancel, or if he was just going to stand me up completely. My shoulder muscles coiled tightly, sending a twinge of pain all the way up my neck. Yeah. I could use a little pampering on a day like this.

"You're right," I said. "I'm definitely not moving fast enough."

I grabbed my phone and shoved it in my bag.

"That's my girl," Tiffany said with a grin.

"When did you guys come up with this plan?" I asked. I slid my arms into the sleeves of my coat and lifted my hair out from under the collar, letting it fall loose down my back.

"Roughly five minutes after your minor breakdown in chapel the other day," Tiffany said matter-of-factly.

My face burned at the memory as I strode out the door. A couple of people had asked me what the snake thing was all about and I'd told them that I didn't want to talk about it. Meanwhile, those who didn't know me well, or who were already wary about me thanks to my close association with the last two murders and murder victims at Easton, had been giving me a wide-berth on campus, taking out-of-the-way routes across the quad just to avoid passing me directly. It was kind of amusing, actually, but sooner or later, I was going to have to come up with some kind of explanation for my actual friends. I just hoped it would be later, because my tired brain was not functioning at high levels these days.

"Five minutes? Try five seconds," Rose said with a laugh. She fell into step behind me as I led the way down the carpeted hallway to the stairs. "She was on her phone making a reservation before the applause had even died down."

I shook my head and jogged down the stairs, shoving open the door and taking a deep breath of the crisp, cold air. Waiting for us at the curb in front of the huge, stone fountain, was a sleek, black town car.

"What would I do without you guys?" I asked as Tiffany slung her arm over my shoulders.

"You'd definitely be in a straitjacket by now," she joked. "Let's roll."

TENSION

"For a young girl, you certainly hold a lot of tension in your shoulders," my masseuse, Kristianne, told me as she finished up my deep tissue massage.

"She has more stress than the usual sixteen-year-old," Rose said, her voice muffled since her face, like mine, was mashed into a donut pillow.

They had no idea how much more stress. Even though the masseuses had told us to leave all electronic devices in the lockers with the rest of our clothes and personal items, I had managed to sneak my iPhone in and half-camouflage it under a towel on the chair in the corner. Every chance I got, I glanced casually in that direction to check if it had lit up with a text while I wasn't paying attention. So far, it had been dormant.

"Okay, Reed," Kristianne said in her quiet, soothing voice. "You can roll over."

Kristianne held up the thick towel and blanket that were covering me, shielding my naked body from her view so I could roll onto my back. My head felt heavy and my brain was all fuzzy and relaxed. Even with the specter of my phone looming in the room, I had somehow managed to let a bit of my tension go.

"How was it?" Tiffany asked from the next bed.

"Amazing," I replied. "Thanks, Kristianne. Thanks, you guys, for bringing me."

"Anytime," Rose said, rolling over as well.

"Okay. We'll leave you girls now," Rose's masseuse, Joanna, said, standing with the other two near the door. They all wore cream-colored polo tops and khaki pants, like some kind of neutral relaxation brigade. "You're free to enjoy lunch in the garden room, and remember to drink lots of water. It will help you flush out all the toxins."

"We will," Tiffany said, taking a deep breath with her eyes closed. "We're good little toxin flushers."

Rose snorted a laugh and the three masseuses exchanged an amused glance before walking out and leaving us to ourselves. I followed Tiffany's example and just lay there for a moment, eyes closed, breathing in the soothing eucalyptus-scented candles and listening to the softly pinging guitar music. This was the one of the greatest gifts anyone could have given me. Why couldn't Josh see how amazing my friends were? It wasn't like he was running around trying to de-stress my chi and loosen my pressure points. Or whatever it was they did around here for a hundred bucks an hour.

"Okay. I'm starving," Tiffany said, sitting up straight. "Let's eat!"

Rose and I grabbed our soft terry cloth robes. Tiffany went to the cooler of cucumber water in the corner and filled three glasses, and Rose went to work securing her hair in a bun. While their backs were turned, I grabbed my phone from under the towel, turned it on to vibrate, and slid it into one of the pockets.

"For you, my dear," Tiffany said, handing me a glass of water.

I downed it in a few gulps and refilled it.

"Wow. Thirsty?" Rose said.

I smiled. "I also have more toxins than your average sixteen-year-old," I joked.

Together we walked out the side door of our "serenity room" and followed the signs pointing the way to the Garden Room. The large, airy space was dotted with small café tables, and three walls were made up of floor-to-ceiling windows, looking out over the bare trees behind the spa. A babbling brook cut its way through the snow, and overhead, white clouds raced their way across a clear, blue sky.

"So, Reed," Rose said as we chose a table and glanced over the menu. It was all salads and fruits and teas. "What really happened with that whole snake thing? Did someone put you up to it?"

"Kind of," I replied.

I had been expecting this question for the past two days, of course, and on the ride over I'd finally put the finishing touches on my cover story. I took a sip of my water, while Tiffany and Rose waited expectantly.

"I lost a bet with Gage," I said, rolling my eyes and faking an embarrassed smile. The whole snake episode was just childish enough to be a brainstorm of his. "I said he couldn't knot the stem of a cherry with his tongue. He did it five times in a row."

"Omigod, Reed! You should know better than to ever make a bet with Gage!" Rose chided me.

"Especially when it involves his tongue," Tiffany added, sticking hers out slightly.

"Lesson learned," I replied. "I will never go there again."

"What can I get for you ladies?" the waitress asked in the same hushed tone everyone seemed to use around here.

"Mango chicken salad, please," I said, leaning back in my chair.

I took a deep breath, secure in the knowledge that neither Tiffany nor Rose would ever catch me in my latest lie. Neither of them was particularly friendly with Gage, and the whole bet story was forgettable enough that by tomorrow neither of them would care anymore. Everything was going to be fine. I was even starting to enjoy myself.

And then my cell phone vibrated.

"What was that?" Rose asked, looking around.

"My phone," I whispered.

I fumbled it out of my pocket and held it under the table.

"Reed! You're not supposed to have that in here," Tiffany hissed, glancing over her shoulder at one of the waitresses.

"What're they going to do, kick me out?" I asked. I pushed back from the table slightly to see the text on the screen. All at once, my lungs filled with relief. The text was from Josh. It read:

Hope we're still on for tonight. I'll pick you up at 8! XO

Thank goodness. I wasn't sure that, on top of everything else, I could handle him dumping me on Valentine's Day.

"It's from Josh," I explained.

Tiffany and Rose nodded knowingly.

I was just about to slide the phone back in my pocket when it vibrated again, startling the breath out of me.

This text was *not* from Josh.

ONLY ONE ASSIGNMENT LEFT. YOU FAIL, SHE DIES. FURTHER INSTRUCTIONS TONIGHT.

And just like that, the shoulder knots Kristianne had worked so hard to uncoil were back.

JUST US

"Ow! Lorna! You stepped on my foot!" Amberly whined. "Ow! Owwww! Astrid! Stop! You're smacking me in the back of the head with your brush."

"Sorry, love," Astrid said. She turned around too quickly and elbowed Amberly in the eye.

"Ow! Crap! Crappity crap crap!" Amberly blurted, doubling over.

"Oh my God, Amberly! Are you okay?" I asked, jumping up from my desk chair. Not that it was easy to do, what with the crowd of Billings Girls milling around in my tiny single room. I shoved by Portia, got a mouthful of hair spray as I ducked by Vienna, and cornered Amberly near the door, where she clutched her hand over her right eye, bent at the waist. Normally, Amberly wasn't my favorite person, but she was one of us now—a true Billings Girl, and I had started to see her as a kind of annoying, precocious little sister. Also, that jab had looked pretty bad.

"No, I'm not okay!" she groused, pushing her blond mane back from her pretty, elfin face. "I miss Billings! Do you remember how big the rooms were? We could have all fit in Noelle's room *with* our dates. And taken group pictures! And had champagne!"

Around me, the other Billings girls sighed nostalgically.

"This is pathetic," Amberly said, throwing up a hand. "And now I have a black eye."

"Here. Let me see." I tugged her hand away from her eye and she blinked a few times. "It's not black. It's just watery and . . . slightly pink," I told her. "Hey. It matches your dress."

"You think?" Amberly asked, looking down at her dark pink silk frock. There wasn't much she loved more than matching her accessories to her clothes.

I laughed. "You're gonna be fine."

"Knock, knock!" Trey Prescott stuck his head into my room. Just opening the door slightly, he practically flattened me and Amberly against the wall. "Damn. It's like a sardine can in here. Fine sardines, don't get me wrong. But still." He found Astrid in the center of the mayhem and smiled. "You ready, baby?"

"I'm *always* ready!" Astrid said, grabbing her sequined clutch. She had to raise her arms over her head and turn sideways to get through the bevy of girls and out the door. The multilayered taffeta and netting on the skirt of her black dress snagged on the beads lining Portia's mini, but she twirled once and broke free. "Ta, ladies!" she sang.

"Hey, Amberly. Hunter's out here too," Trey said.

"Yeeee!" Amberly whirled around to double-check her eyes in the full-length mirror.

"Wait. You're going to the dance with Hunter Braden?" I asked her, a sour taste rising up in the back of my throat. Hunter and I had gone on exactly one seriously awful date last fall, an experience I didn't exactly relish for Amberly.

"Uh, yeah? The hottest guy in school asks you to the Valentine's Day dance, you say yes," Amberly replied.

I rolled my eyes and patted her on the back as I practically shoved her out the door. "Good luck with that one."

She didn't even seem to hear me as she joined him in the hallway and he helped her on with her coat. That was Hunter for you. A consummate gentleman. For five minutes. When that space of time had passed, all bets were off. I knew from experience.

"Well, at least there's more room in here, now," I said, returning to the makeup mirror on my desk.

"Hey, Reed, is this your brother?" Lorna asked, picking up a framed family portrait from atop my dresser. "He's hot."

"Yeah. And unfortunately, he knows it," I replied, reaching for a red lip gloss that looked like it would match my dress.

"You don't want that one. It's got orange undertones," Ivy said, grabbing it out of my hand. "It'll clash."

My stomach turned and I avoided her gaze. She had to be here because all the BLS members had decided to come over, but I still had a feeling she had something to do with Noelle's disappearance. Just being around her was making my skin prickle.

"Here. Try this."

She handed me her own lip gloss with a smile.

"No, thanks," I said, tossing it back to her. "I think I'll just go neutral."

Ivy eyed me for a second, as if she sensed something was up, but then shrugged. "Whatever you say."

"Your dad is cute too. For an old guy," Lorna said. She looked at me over the top of the photograph. "But you guys look nothing alike."

"Everyone always says that," I replied. "I look like my mom and Scott looks like my dad."

"Which is probably a good thing," Kiki joked, leaning over my shoulder to fluff her hair in my mirror. "Otherwise you'd have a five o'clock shadow and he'd have those delicate cheekbones of yours," she said, giving my cheek a pinch.

"Hey, Ivy! You in here?" Gage shoved open the door, slamming it into Vienna's foot. She fell against the side of my dresser, grabbed her injured toes, and let out a string of curses worthy of a backstage Kanye outburst.

"Dude. Watch where you're standing," Gage said.

"You suck, Gage Coolidge," Vienna said, hopping over to my bed to check for bleeding. Her dark gray strapless dress barely restrained her breasts, and for a second there, I was sure one or both was going to pop out. Which, of course, Gage would have loved.

"Only on certain body parts," he replied, giving her a lecherous glance.

"Ew!" Portia, Rose, and Tiffany exclaimed as one.

"Ah, my date. I couldn't be more proud," Ivy said. She dropped
her lip gloss back in her purse and joined Gage at the door. "See you
guys there!"

Portia rolled her eyes as the door slammed behind them. "If those
two were any more off-again-on-again they'd be a light switch."

A few of the girls giggled, but I felt a knot growing in my chest.
Were Ivy and Gage really back together, or was he just a beard for her
real man—Tattoo Guy? Or maybe Tattoo Guy wasn't a boyfriend at all.
Maybe he was only in Ivy's life to help her wreak havoc on mine and
Noelle's.

I turned back to my reflection and reached for my original lip gloss
again, trying not to think about it. Tonight was supposed to be fun.
Romantic. It was supposed to be about me and Josh. If only I could
manage to stop obsessing about Noelle's kidnapping and my ability to
save her for more than five minutes.

There was another knock at the door. One by one, all the hottest guys of Easton showed up to squire my friends off to the dance.
Weston Bright was Tiffany's date, Jason Darlington came for Vienna,
Dominic Infante picked up Portia, and Marc Alberro, much to my
delight, arrived for Kiki. Finally, Carson Levere, who was a year
younger than us, but smart and insanely cute, showed up clutching a
dozen red roses to claim Lorna, and Rose and I were left alone.

As Lorna closed the door behind her, I felt a thump of foreboding.
Maybe Josh wasn't coming for me after all.

"Is Damon coming up here?" I asked.

"Nah. New Hathaway rule. Apparently since he's an off-campus date, he's not allowed inside the dorms, so I told him I'd just meet him at the hotel," Rose said, perching on the edge of my bed. "But I'll wait for Josh with you."

Might be a long wait, I thought, glancing at my phone. It was already 8:15. Not hugely late. Unless you lived a thirty-second walk away from your date, of course. But the last shuttle over to the Driscoll Hotel in Easton was supposed to leave at eight thirty. What if he didn't get here in time? Or at all?

Then, just like that, there was a knock at the door. Both Rose and I stood, and I smoothed the skirt of my red satin dress.

"Come in!"

Josh opened the door with a smile. "Sorry I'm late. Would you believe some freshman outside asked me to tie his tie for him?"

Rose and I laughed and Josh produced a single red rose from behind his back. "Happy Valentine's Day."

"I think I'll leave you two alone," Rose said, reaching for her coat, which was folded at the end of my bed. "See you there!"

I smiled and twiddled my fingers at her as she slipped out. Josh wrapped his arms around me and gave me a long kiss on the lips. "I hate that we've been fighting," he said.

"Me too," I replied, letting out a sigh of relief. "Let's not do that anymore."

"Deal," Josh replied. "Tonight is not about suspects or intrigue or kidnappers. Tonight is about you." He gave me a kiss on one shoulder. "And me." He kissed the other shoulder. "And the dance." Then he kissed me, once more, on the lips.

Suddenly, I didn't feel like going anywhere. I just wanted to stay right there in my room all night, with him. But I knew we had to at least make an appearance at the dance. Otherwise everyone would freak out, wondering where we were. Besides, I wanted to congratulate Constance on what I was sure would be a job well done.

"Come on," I said, taking Josh's hand. "Let's get this dance thing over with so we can come back here and make out."

He laughed. "I like the way you think."

We walked out of the room together. As I reached back to close the door, I caught a glimpse of my phone, sitting on my desk. My heart skipped a tense beat. I couldn't believe I'd almost forgotten my lifeline to Noelle.

"Hang on a sec," I said.

Leaving Josh in the hall, I went back inside and grabbed the phone. As I picked it up, it let out a loud beep. My pulse skidded to a stop. I had a text. Quickly, I opened the message. It read, simply:

YOUR FINAL ASSIGNMENT: BREAK UP WITH JOSH HOLLIS. IN PUBLIC.

PUBLIC BREAKUP

Constance had done an amazing job. As Josh and I danced, holding each other close at the center of the gleaming hardwood dance floor, I looked around the Driscoll Hotel ballroom, taking it all in. Solidifying in my mind the details of what was bound to be one of the worst nights of my life.

The ballroom had been turned into an otherworldly tunnel of love. Deep red and purple hearts covered every possible surface, in all imaginable textures. There were sequined hearts, fur hearts, lace hearts, silky hearts. Hearts made out of paper and netting and beads and dried flowers. The ceiling was home to thousands of dark red balloons and the DJ's glass booth had been filled with millions of candy hearts. Waiters and waitresses circled the room with heart-shaped trays full of chocolate-covered strawberries, pink-frosted cupcakes, and Shirley Temple drinks. Everywhere I looked, couples danced close together, touching noses, touching lips, touching everywhere.

It was all a cruel joke.

"Hey. Is everything okay?" Josh said in my ear.

I flinched, startled, and pulled back to look at him. We were surrounded by our coupled-off friends. Skirts swished, ties were loosened. Everyone was having a romantic good time.

"Everything's fine. Why?" I asked, my voice thick.

"You're kind of clutching my neck," Josh said, tilting his head.

I removed my hand and looked at my palm, resting my forearm on his shoulder. My fingers were red, and my palm was clammy. Guess that's what happens when you're trying to cling to something you have to let go of.

Josh looked down at me quizzically. My heart seemed to pound from inside my stomach. Even though it was cool in the cavernous room, sweat prickled the back of my neck. I looked around at the smiling faces of my friends—Tiffany cracking up over something Kiki had just said, Portia looking hopefully up at Dominic as they danced, Constance over in the corner with Walt Whittaker at her side, nodding and grinning as Headmaster Hathaway congratulated her. It was so unfair. Everyone was so happy and carefree and here I was, hiding yet another deep, dark secret, being forced to give up the one person who made me feel safe and loved. The one person I could trust.

I looked up into Josh's incredible green eyes. This was going to be the hardest thing I ever had to do. Once again I had to wonder what these kidnappers were thinking. Why weren't they out there trying to extort millions from Noelle's parents? Why, instead, did they choose to torture me?

Because this was personal. That was the only explanation. This was not about money. This was about me and Noelle. About punishing us. It was the only explanation.

Just do it, Reed! A little voice in my head shouted—a voice that sounded a lot like Noelle's. *Just do it and get it over with.*

I swallowed hard and took a step back. Cold air rushed between us like a wall of ice.

"Actually, everything's not okay," I said loudly. They had, after all, said I was to do this in public. It wouldn't be very public if no one noticed.

Josh blinked, understandably confused. One second I'm clinging to him so tightly I'm leaving finger marks in his skin. The next I'm backing away and unnecessarily shouting.

"What is it?" he said, his voice considerably softer than mine. He closed the gap between us and reached for my hand. "Is it Noelle?" he asked. "Have you heard something?"

Tears stung my eyes. He was so caring. So unselfish. We'd promised this night would not be about the Noelle drama, but here he was, bringing it up, just because he thought it was upsetting me.

"No," I said, yanking my hand away. "It's not that. I . . . Josh, listen. I'm sorry," I said, raising my voice again. "I'm sorry to do this on Valentine's Day, but it's over."

All the color washed right out of Josh's face, but he still eyed me dubiously. A few people around us stopped dancing. The whispers began, starting in the center of the room and whooshing out to all corners, like ripples in otherwise calm waters.

"You're joking, right? This is some kind of prank." He looked around as if waiting for a clown to step out and hit him in the face with a whipped cream pie.

"No," I said. "No, I'm not."

"What are you talking about?" he asked with a strained smile. "You can't—"

"I'm talking about us," I interrupted. "We're over."

The smile dropped away and his face started to grow red. All I wanted to do was grab him and tell him he was right. It *was* a prank. That it was all going to be fine. I couldn't bear that I was doing this to him.

"What?" Josh blurted.

Tiffany and West backed up a little, giving us space, as if they thought Josh was going to wrestle me to the ground.

"I can't . . . I just can't be with you anymore," I said.

From the corner of my eye, I saw someone approaching. I was so surprised to see someone moving toward us rather than away, I must have flinched, because Josh turned around to see what I was looking at. It was Sawyer. He had just emerged from the crowd, and he couldn't have picked a worse moment. The second Josh saw him he let out a strangled sort of laugh.

"Is this about him?" he asked, his jaw set as he turned to face me again.

"What?" I said, my voice cracking. "No. Sawyer and I are just—"

"Then is it that Upton guy?" Josh demanded. "I saw that note he sent you. Does he always go around calling other guys' girlfriends 'beautiful' and signing his letters 'love'?"

Actually, yeah, he kind of does, I thought automatically. And how the hell had Josh seen that note? But then my brain remembered I was in kind of an end-of-my-world drama here.

"Josh, I'm sorry. I just—"

"I can't believe this," Josh said, glancing around wildly, as if he couldn't even look at me for a second longer. He pushed both hands into his hair, holding it back with his palms to his temples, as if he were trying to keep his brain from exploding. "You're not really doing this."

He dropped his hands again and looked at me imploringly. I said nothing. I couldn't. There was nothing in me to say. Then he blinked and for a split second my heart caught. He knew! It was right there in his eyes. He knew why I was doing this. He knew it was all a ruse. He knew the kidnappers had set me up.

But then he covered his face for a moment and when he looked at me again, his face was red and he was fuming. I realized with a sinking sensation that I had just imagined it. Wishful thinking.

"You'd better be really sure about this, Reed," Josh snapped. "Because if this is it, this is really it. You do this right now and I'm done. For good."

My hands were shaking. My knees quivered beneath me. Every cell in my body cried out for me to take it back. To step into his arms. To let him hold me. I loved him so much, my body was physically revolting against my words. I felt like I was going to throw up, crumble, pass out, die.

But then I saw Noelle in my mind's eye. Panicked. Bleeding.

Possibly even dying. This was just a breakup, but she really could die. If I didn't do this, they would kill her.

"Is this what you really want?" Josh demanded.

I looked around at the crowd. It seemed as if the entire school was watching. If the kidnappers wanted public, they were certainly getting public. I saw my friends huddled together—Tiffany, Portia, Rose, Vienna, Kiki, Lorna, Astrid, and Amberly—all of them watching us, gaping, baffled. Only Ivy was alone, off to the side, her expression completely unreadable.

Is this what you wanted? I thought, glaring at her. *Well, I hope you're enjoying the show.*

I wanted to storm over there, grab her by the hair, and wrest her to the floor. I wanted to make her tell me what she knew. Make her suffer the way Josh and I were both suffering right now. But I was not going to give her the satisfaction of cracking.

Still, I swore to myself at that moment that if she did turn out to be the kidnapper, I was going to make her pay for this. Big-time.

"Yes," I said firmly, looking Josh in the eye. "This is what I really want."

Josh's face was slack. He was nothing but a gray, sagging mask of his former self. After everything I'd put him through, that crap with Dash, the shooting, everything, this was clearly the worst thing I could have done.

I expected him to scream at me one last time. To tell me off. To call me a whore or a bitch or a psycho. Any one of these things would have actually made me feel better.

But instead he simply turned around and walked away.

LIVING THE NIGHTMARE

Right, so, where the hell was Noelle? I'd done everything these jack-asses had asked of me. Four assignments set, four assignments complete. Didn't that mean I'd won? Didn't that mean I was supposed to get some kind of information on Noelle's whereabouts? I'd been up all night, sitting straight up on my bed with my phone in my lap, waiting. Waiting for the information on how to save my friend. I'd even changed into jeans and boots and a black sweater, packed an overnight bag, and charged my phone, primed and ready for a trek through the snow or a train trip to Boston or a flight to Siberia. But nothing had come. It was all silence. All night long.

Every once in a while, I found myself staring at the wall between my room and Ivy's, my jaw clenched, my fingers curled into fists. I couldn't stop thinking about the expression on her face as she watched me break up with Josh. At first I hadn't been able to place what it was. I'd been so wrapped up in my own pain, my own regret, my own despair. But the more I thought about it, the more it looked like . . . satisfaction. Like pride over a job well-done. Like she'd been expecting it to happen, just waiting to revel in the end result.

Josh had insisted Ivy couldn't be behind this, but had anyone ever suspected that Ariana had killed Thomas? Hadn't we all been sucked in by Sabine's innocent act? If I was going on history here, it *had* to be Ivy. Somehow, the people that I thought were my best friends, always turned out to be my worst enemies.

Part of me wanted to bang on the wall. Part of me wanted to just walk in there and shake her, demand to know where Noelle was. But I kept stopping myself. Because what if I was wrong? I didn't think I'd be able to live with myself.

By three o'clock in the morning I was pissed and pacing my tiny cell of a room. Why had I done all of this? Why had I made Upton fly to France? Why had I risked getting arrested in Sweet Nothings and humiliated myself in front the entire school and broken up with the love of my life? *Why*? For what purpose? Was it just some kind of game to these people? Were they out there somewhere just laughing at me?

Was Ivy sitting in the next room right now, laughing at me?

By five a.m. I was desperate, talking to the phone as if I could make it text me itself. "Come on, you stupid thing. Where is she? Tell me where Noelle is! Just effing tell me!"

Shockingly, that didn't work.

So now, here I was, sitting in the library, my head heavy, my eyes even heavier, but my heart pounding as if I'd just sprinted a marathon. I had thought that getting out of my room would help. That it would distract me from my misery and despair, but I was wrong. Sitting at the end of a wide oak table, some history books open in front of me for show, I was just reminded of how low I had sunk. All around me, life went on. Study groups poured over notebooks and projects. Students tapped away at laptops. A couple of girls flipped through the latest gossip magazine, laughing over stars and their cellulite. Over in the corner, Marc and Kiki smooched in a study carrel, pretending no one could see them, all flush and gooey with the stink of new love.

I just wanted to rip my heart out and throw it at them.

Everything was just as it was supposed to be. This was the way Easton Academy had appeared to me in the catalog a year and a half ago. The glossy, autumn-hued catalog that had seduced me into applying, that had practically guaranteed a better life. I had envisioned a world where beautiful people strolled cobblestone paths, debating politics and laughing over the events of the day. I saw huddles of kids hanging out in the library, analyzing poetry, defending their theses, celebrating new discoveries. I had even conjured up images of me and some gorgeous, preppy boyfriend, walking hand in hand after winning our respective soccer games, chasing windblown leaves down the hill as we headed for dinner with our friends at the dining hall.

And maybe I'd had a few of these spare moments since I'd been here, but they had been few and far between. And they had always ended in misery.

Everyone around me was living in the Easton Academy from the catalog. They were living the dream. But me? I was living a nightmare. Over and over and over again. Full of death and near death and stalking and backstabbing and kidnapping and pain. I just wanted things to be normal. I just wanted all the drama to stop.

I simply wanted my friend back, safe and sound.

And still, my phone was silent on the table. It looked like the nightmare was never going to end.

INNER BITCH

My hands shook as I held my hands under the steaming hot water in the Pemberly bathroom that night. The water in there had exactly two temperatures: arctic bitter and scalding hot. Tonight was definitely a night for scalding. The temperature outside had dipped well below freezing and the wind chill was in the single digits. Besides, cold water wasn't exactly going to stop the trembling, which I was more than frantic to stop. It couldn't be healthy for one's entire body to be as frenetic as mine had been for the past twenty-four hours.

I dipped my head forward and splashed my face with the hot water. As I stood up straight again, my phone, sitting on the small silver shelf in front of the mirror, beeped. I snatched it and it slipped right out of my wet hand, crashing to the floor.

"Frak!" I said through my teeth.

At that moment, Ivy walked into the room. She took one look at my dripping face, then grabbed the phone up off the floor and handed it to me.

"You okay?" she asked.

I snatched the phone and took a step back. Was her appearance at that moment just a coincidence? Had she just sent a text about Noelle from the hallway then walked in here to gauge my reaction?

I looked down at the screen. It was a text from Constance. My heart ricocheted off in a whole new direction. Constance was texting me again? It read:

Sry bout U + Josh. Hope everythings ok. X C

I pressed my lips together to keep a whole new wave of emotion at bay. Tossing the phone back on the shelf, I grabbed my towel and dried my face, taking an extra moment to breathe in the Tide-scented softness. When I lowered the towel again, Ivy was staring at me.

"What?" I snapped.

I turned to look at myself in the mirror. Water splotches dotted my Penn State sweatshirt and my skin was the color of pea soup. All of these things with Ivy . . . they couldn't all be coincidences. They just couldn't. Standing there with her breathing over my shoulder, my frustration mounted and mounted and mounted, like hot lava rising up inside of me. Any second, I was going to blow.

"Nothing!" Ivy said, clearly offended. She dropped her basket of toiletries on the shelf and turned the water on over the sink next to mine. "Could you be any more on edge?"

"Oh, please," I blurted. "Don't give me the innocent act."

Ivy glanced at me in the mirror. "What are you talking about?"

"I know what you're doing, Ivy," I said, shoving my toothbrush and toothpaste back into my own toiletry kit shakily. "And you're not going to get away with it."

Ivy turned to look at me, her dark eyes wide. "What am I doing, Reed? Seriously. Tell me. Because if you're going to suck me into one of your paranoid delusions, I think I have the right to know the details."

"I'm not paranoid!" I shouted, trembling from head to toe.

"Is this about Josh?" Ivy said, turning off the water. "Because whatever happened between the two of you, I had nothing to do with it. Gage and I are back together, so you can just stop thinking everyone wants what you've got."

"Oh, really? Gage is your new boyfriend now? Not Tattoo Guy?" I demanded, my chest heaving.

Ivy's eyes narrowed. "What are you, spying on me now?"

"Who needs to spy? You're the one parading that freak show around campus all the time!"

Ivy took a deep breath and jutted her bottom teeth out for a second, as if she was steeling herself. "Okay, first of all, KC is not a freak show. He's one of my best friends from home and he's been hanging around here because his dad is on a permanent bender and he needs me," she snapped. "And secondly, where do you get off walking around here like the entire world revolves around you? Like you can say anything to anyone and then act like everything's fine? Well, guess what, Reed? It's not fine. You can't just suddenly start treating me like shit and then expect me to be your friend again the next day."

My nostrils flared. "I haven't been treating you like—"

"Yes," she said with a bitter laugh. "You have. Avoiding me? Shooting me looks? Refusing my lip gloss like I have herpes or something? And now this?" She whipped her toiletry kit down off the shelf, where it slammed against the sink with a loud clatter. "You didn't even tell me you were thinking about breaking up with Josh. You didn't even talk to me about it, and I thought we were supposed to be best friends."

I blinked. For the first time since she'd walked through the door, I started doubting whether she even knew Noelle was really missing.

"Ivy, you don't under—"

"No. I don't want to hear it," she said, lifting her free hand. "I'm done, Reed. Don't talk to me again until you've had your inner bitch surgically removed."

Then she turned around and stormed out, slamming the bathroom door behind her.

A LITTLE HELP

"Hey, Reed. How's the extra-credit project going?"

I blinked a few times, slowly pulling myself out of my deep, dark daze. Tiffany, Portia, and Rose all hovered around my marble-topped table in the solarium, toting steaming coffees and yummy-smelling scones. Slowly, I looked down at my laptop. There was nothing on the screen in front of me other than a lonely, blinking cursor.

"Um, not good," I said.

Portia pulled out a chair and placed her plate down. "How NG are we talking? VNG or BNG?"

My brow knit. Sometimes, talking to Portia was like trying to decode a secret spy message from the CIA.

"Um, BNG?" I said. "That's beyond not good, right?"

"What can we do to help?" Tiffany asked, taking the chair across from Portia. Rose sat down across from me, her diminutive frame pretty much disappearing behind my laptop screen.

"Oh, you guys don't have to—"

"It's due tomorrow, isn't it?" Rose asked, sitting up straight so I could at least see her blue eyes over the monitor.

"Yeah," I said miserably. Where had the last week gone? Oh yeah. It had flown by with me running around at the beck-and-call of some crazed lunatic who didn't even feel the need to reward me for my efforts by telling me how to save my friend.

"Then let us help," Tiffany said. "History's Portia's best subject."

"Aside from finance," Portia said, lifting her chin.

"It's true. Mr. Barber worships her," Rose put in, taking a sip of her coffee. "Remember that presentation you did on the influence of first ladies on international policy? I thought he was going to drop down on one knee and propose to you right there."

"Okay, ew," Portia said with a shudder.

"Girl's holding out for a bona fide prince, remember?" Tiffany said, her eyes sparkling as she lifted her coffee mug to her lips.

"Preferably a western European one," Portia confirmed. She shrugged out of her fur-lined jacket and rested her elbows on the table, her gold necklaces glinting in the light from overhead. "But Rose is right. I am the only person in the history of Easton Academy ever to earn an A-plus from the Barber."

I frowned, duly impressed.

"Come on, Reed. No one could be expected to concentrate on extra credit at a time like this," Tiffany said, referring to my breakup with Josh, of course, not to Noelle's suspended fate. "Just tell us what you need and we'll do it. Delegate."

"You're sure?" I said, sitting up a bit straighter.

"You need to learn how to accept a little help," Portia said, tossing her dark hair over her shoulder. "You don't have to do everything yourself, FYI."

"And what else is the Billings Literary Society for?" Rose asked slyly, arching one eyebrow. "I mean, if not to support one another academically."

I felt a smile tug at my lips and the sensation was very odd, but very welcome. "Okay, I'm supposed to write an article as if I'm a reform journalist, covering the breakup of the Standard Oil Company," I said. "So first . . . I need to find out what, exactly, the Standard Oil Company was. Also, it'd probably be good to know why it broke up."

"Wow. You really do need help," Portia said. "I'm on research!"

She pulled her own laptop out of her bag and moved her coffee and blueberry scone to the next table to make room for it.

"I'll pull up some of Ida Tarbell's articles so you can get an idea of the writing style of the day," Rose offered, producing her laptop as well.

"Okay, we're getting a little crowded here," Tiffany said. She got up and moved all her stuff to the next table, then pulled out her sleek, silver MacBook. "I'll do photo research."

"Photo research?" I asked.

"Yeah. You need to set this up so it looks like an actual article," Portia said, as if this was entirely obvious to the world. "Barber will *love* that."

"It's too bad we're not in with Constance anymore. She could typeset it at the newspaper office and make it look really authentic," Rose said, screwing up her mouth.

"I could always ask Marc," I interjected, feeling an actual flicker of academic excitement. It was dim, but it was there. "Maybe he could even print it out on newspaper stock."

"If you can get him to remove his lips from Kiki's for more than five seconds," Portia replied, her fingers flying over her keyboard. "Those two are totally gunning for the PDA award."

I sat back in my chair as the three of them feverishly got to work. Suddenly my heart was full to overflowing. My friends were the best. Hands down, the best friends on earth.

"What am I supposed to do?" I asked, feeling a tad guilty.

"Here." Tiffany handed me her plate, which was full of chocolate biscotti, never taking her eyes off her screen. "Eat chocolate, read up on the Standard Oil Company, and try to come up with a snazzy headline."

I laughed and placed the plate down on top of my keyboard. I could take a break for the amount of time it took to devour one biscotti, couldn't I? I took a bite, the chocolate coating melting in my mouth. For a split second I started to feel better, like maybe I could actually pull this off, but then Mr. Hathaway had appeared as if from nowhere. He stood right behind Rose, holding a steaming to-go cup of coffee.

"Ladies," he said, his expression suspicious as his gaze slid from one computer to another. He'd already tried to bust the Billings Literary Society once, and he seemed to get tense whenever he saw more than two or three former Billings Girls hanging out together.

After my outburst in chapel and Noelle's continued absence, he was probably starting to suspect that he was somehow being snowed by a bunch of teenage girls. Which, let's face it, he was. "What're we working on?"

"Extra credit," Portia said, unfazed. She reached for her coffee and took a sip, crossing one leg over the other as she gazed up at the headmaster, all cool. "What're *you* working on?"

Tiffany hid a laugh behind her hand. The headmaster gave Portia a tight smile.

"A cinnamon latte," he replied, lifting his cup.

"Nice choice," Portia replied. "I like a man with a sweet tooth, Double H."

For the first time since I'd known him, Mr. Hathaway looked flummoxed. "Thank you, Miss Ahronian, for that entirely inappropriate comment," he said, his face all red.

"DMI," she replied. Then she turned and got back to work.

"Don't mention it," Rose translated helpfully.

"Ah, well. It's nice to see our students being so industrious," Mr. Hathaway said, looking directly at me. "Remember, ladies, if you ever need any help with anything, my door is always open."

My heart skipped a beat as he held my gaze for a long moment. "Good night, ladies."

"Night!" my friends called after him as he strolled off.

As soon as he was a safe distance away, they all cracked up over Portia's brazen behavior.

"I don't think Double H has any royalty in his blood, P," Tiffany said.

"But my, is he hot," Portia said, watching him go. "For a geriatric," she added, earning another round of laughter.

Meanwhile, my eyes followed Mr. Hathaway, my breath coming short and shallow as he wove his way around the crowded tables, stopping to talk to a group of students. It had been two days since I'd completed my fourth assignment for the kidnappers. Two days and no word. Two days Noelle might have spent out there somewhere alone and scared, clinging to life by a thread.

Maybe Josh had been right all along. Maybe I needed to tell someone what was going on. Especially now that I'd done my part and it had gotten me nowhere. So what if the kidnappers had warned me not to tell anyone? They'd also told me that if I completed four tasks for them, Noelle would be fine, and they hadn't exactly come through there. And Headmaster Hathaway had said I could trust him.

But could I? I hadn't exactly proven to be the best judge of character in the past.

He was at the door of the solarium and was about to walk out. My heart made the decision for me as I suddenly found myself jumping to my feet. My chair scraped against the marble floor as I shoved it behind me.

"I'll be right back," I told my friends, ignoring their surprised looks.

I caught up to the headmaster in the wide, carpeted hallway just outside the solarium. A group of sophomore girls milled around on the other side of the hall, texting and laughing as they checked out one another's phones.

"Headmaster!" I blurted.

He turned around, his eyebrows raised, surprised to see me gasping for breath behind him.

"Reed," he said.

I swallowed hard, just hoping . . . praying I was doing the right thing. "I was wondering . . . can I talk to you about something?" I glanced sidelong at the gigglers. "Somewhere . . . else?"

The headmaster squared off with me, rounding his shoulders. "Sure. Everything okay?"

"Yes, I just . . . wanted to take you up on your offer," I said.

"Good. That's good," he replied. "Meet me in my office in fifteen minutes."

"Thanks," I replied, already wondering what I was going to tell my friends about bailing on my own homework assignment. Not that they would mind. Clearly, they were all about helping me. And hopefully, what I had to tell Mr. Hathaway wouldn't take long. Hopefully, once I dumped my whole, sad, sordid story on him, he'd jump into action and my work here would be done. Ideally, by the end of tonight, the police would be involved and Noelle would be back home, safe and sound.

SO CLOSE

Five minutes later, I raced across the frigid, deserted campus, my hands clasping my collar closed under my chin, keeping my eyes on the shoveled cobblestone pathway to avoid icy patches. I'd been so distracted that I'd gone out without my hat, scarf, or gloves and now, every inch of my exposed skin screamed out in protest. But even in my discomfort, I already felt at least a hundred times lighter, a hundred times more awake, a hundred times more alive. And at least I was still wearing my big, old, warm boots.

In minutes, I would be unburdened. Hathaway would know all. And yes, I might get punished for forming the Billings Literary Society, but I hardly thought that would be his main focus, what with Noelle's life hanging in the balance and all. Besides, as long as she was found and she was okay, I didn't care if they expelled me from this stupid school.

Sniffling and gasping for breath, I sprinted up the outdoor steps to Hull Hall. My hand had just grabbed the metal door handle when I heard scuffling footsteps behind me. Then, out of nowhere, a large gloved hand reached past my shoulder and shoved the door closed again. I whirled around and found myself face-to-face with a big, burly police officer. The fleece collar of his dark blue jacket was flipped up around his stubbly cheeks and he wore a wool hat low over his brow. His badge was pinned to the left lapel of his coat, and it shone, thanks to the security light above the door.

"Reed Brennan?" he said gruffly.

Behind him, two other officers scurried up, out of breath. Had something happened to my family? To Josh? Was this about Noelle?

"Yes?" I said.

The officer whipped out a pair of handcuffs, grabbed me by the arm, and swung me around in one, swift motion. I was so surprised I went temporarily blank, my vision blurring over and my head going weightless. He lifted my bag off my shoulder and tossed it down the stairs, where one of his buddies caught it. Then the cold metal closed around my wrists.

I was being handcuffed. *Why* was I being handcuffed?

"Wait!" I blurted, finding my voice. My heart spiraled around in my chest like a tilt-a-whirl gone horribly off the track. "What're you doing? What's going—"

"Reed Brennan," the cop said in my ear, "you are under arrest for the murder of Noelle Lange."

THE FIFTH ASSIGNMENT

Noelle is not dead. She's not. She's not, she's not, she's not.

"You have the right to remain silent," the cop said, grasping my shoulders and flinging me around. My stomach swooped as my foot slid off the top step in front of Hull Hall. I stumbled forward, down the stairs, and right into the waiting arms of the other two officers. One was short, fat, male, and whose breath smelled like cheese. The other was a scrawny woman with dark hair and a zit on her chin the size of Plymouth Rock. "Anything you say can and will be used against you in a court of law."

"No, no, no, no wait!" I shouted. My mind reeled in ten different directions as the cops dragged me to my feet by my upper arms. I looked around for someone, anyone, to see me—to help—but there was no one around. "What happened? Where did you find her?"

"Kid, I'm not supposed to say this," the gruff cop said, straightening his gloves as he descended the stairs after me. "But you really might want to remain silent."

Cheese Breath and Zit Lady pulled me forward, manhandling me around the corner and to the back of Hull Hall, where an unmarked police car waited, idling in the small, faculty-only parking lot. I wrenched my neck, trying to look over my shoulder at the window of Headmaster Hathaway's office. I could see that the light was on and I willed him to look outside. To save me just like I'd been hoping he'd save Noelle.

But now, Noelle could not be saved. Because now, Noelle was dead.

Just like Thomas. Just like Cheyenne. Visions of funerals and wakes and black clothes and dark limousines and bawling friends flashed through my mind. Visions of a life without Noelle. It wasn't possible. It was not possible.

I wanted my mom.

"Wait," I said. "You can't just take me. You have to tell the headmaster. You have to call my parents."

"Done and done, kid," the original cop said. Zit Lady got into the back seat and slid all the way to the opposite door, while Cheese Breath shoved my head down and practically kicked me in the shin to get me to join his friend. As I bounced onto the seat, I felt my phone in the back pocket of my jeans. I'd started to keep it there for the last couple of days, so I'd be sure to always have it on me. "We're going to the station."

Then, the door slammed. "She's not dead," I said, as the lead cop sat down behind the steering wheel. Cheese Breath dropped down next to him and picked up a fast-food drink from the floor to take a nice, long sip. How could he suck down root beer at a time like this? "She can't be dead. Tell me where you found her. Tell me what's going on."

But they merely slammed their doors and then, just like that, we were peeling off into the night, leaving the lights of Easton Academy winking in the rearview mirror.

I sat back in the seat and tried to breathe, the muscles of my upper arms crying out in protest at being forced into such an odd angle. I knew the route to the Easton Police Station well, having been there many times after Thomas's disappearance and Cheyenne's death. I wondered if Detective Hauer still worked there. I practically salivated at the thought of seeing a sympathetic face right then. I needed to talk to someone I knew. Someone who had long since learned that Reed Brennan was not capable of murder.

Murder. Noelle had been murdered. Someone had murdered Noelle. Had it been painful? Had she known it was coming? Had she been scared?

Tears blurred my vision as the car whizzed through the green light at the bottom of Main Street, Easton. I caught a glimpse of the illuminated light posts that marked the front of the Easton police department, halfway up the hill. Suddenly, I was sitting up straight.

"Where're we going?" I asked. "The station is back that way."

I saw Gruff and Cheese Breath exchange a look. Zit Lady sighed and looked out her window.

"No one said we were Easton PD," Gruff said, taking a turn so late the tires squealed. I was flung into Zit Lady's side, and she shoved me off her as the car righted itself again.

My heart was now officially in overdrive. "If you're not Easton PD, then who are you?"

"We're state police," Cheese Breath replied, taking another sip of his soda. "Kidnapping and murder are a bit bigger than local jurisdiction. Now how about you just sit back and shut up?"

I slumped down, feeling as if I'd been slapped. Was it normal for cops to be so outright rude? I'd just found out my best friend was dead. But then, I guess to them I was a murder suspect, which made no sense at all. Noelle had been alive this time last week. I'd seen a video of her. And I had an alibi for pretty much every second of my life since then. Besides, I had no motive, no reason on Earth to kill Noelle. What kind of evidence did these people think they had against me?

"Where are you taking me?" I asked, keeping my voice as even as possible. Outside the window there was nothing but trees. We were on some kind of dark country road with no lights, no gas stations, no nothing. One lone, chipped sign read: SOLDIER WOODS CAMPGROUNDS, 2 MILES.

"That's for us to know and you to find out."

Suddenly, Gruff yanked the wheel to the right and we were on a skinny, one-lane road winding through the woods. After about five minutes, we came to a clearing, and a big, abandoned house loomed in front of us. It looked like something out of a movie about the old south, all white plank siding, slanted roofs, and dormered windows. But all the windows were boarded up, the plank siding was chipped and rotting, and the slanted roof on the north side had completely collapsed. The iron fencing around the snow-covered garden was

bent, battered, and rusted, and the stone steps to the green front door
had crumbled in spots, leaving a pile of debris at their foot.

Gruff stopped the car and the two men in front got out. Zit Lady
stayed where she was, avoiding my gaze, but blocking me from making
a play for her door. Gruff yanked open the door on my side, grabbed
my arm, and dragged me out. Only then did Zit Lady emerge from the
car, jogging ahead to the house. She stepped over the broken bits of
stairs and shoved open the front door.

"What is this?" I demanded, trying to wrench free from Gruff's
grasp. He held firm, tripping me forward toward the house. "Where
are we? Shouldn't we be at a police station right about now?" I asked,
as he guided me up the stairs.

I'd seen enough cop movies to know that this type of unexpected
twist was not good. Were they bringing me here to coerce a confession
out of me?

"Our job was to get you off campus and bring you here, kid. The
FBI guys'll be here any minute to pick you up," Gruff said. He shoved
me through the door, where the old, wooden floorboards creaked
beneath our feet. There was one chair in the center of the parlor room
off to the right and he deposited me onto it. My phone jammed into
my butt cheek and I winced, but no one seemed to notice. There were
no lights on in the place, but the moonlight poured through the huge
windows behind me, lighting the room. It felt even colder in here than
it had outside, as if the heat hadn't been turned on in ages. Still, Gruff
took his hat and gloves off, tossing them atop the half-wall dividing
the parlor from the front hall. His brown hair stood straight up on the

sides as the three of them stood before me, forming a semicircle of stern faces and crossed arms.

"In the meantime, how about you tell us what, exactly, happened to Noelle Lange?" Zit Lady said, speaking for the first time. She walked around behind me and I heard a jangle of keys as she unlocked my handcuffs. As they fell away, I whipped my hands quickly into my lap, savoring the freedom.

"I thought you said I had the right to remain silent," I replied, rubbing my wrists.

"Oh, you do. It's just . . . if you tell us the truth now, we might be able to help you cut a deal later," Zit Lady said, slowly walking around my chair.

My heart started to pound. "I watch *The Closer*, you know. I'm not an idiot. You're trying to get me to confess without a lawyer around."

Zit Lady snorted a laugh. "You don't want to talk, fine. You can tell it all to the FBI when they get here."

My palms started to sweat. *Okay, think, Reed.* What could be the harm in telling them what had really happened? They were the cops, right? Cops didn't want to arrest the wrong person. They wanted to punish the people who actually did the crime. If I told them my story, they'd have to believe it. Because A) it was true, and B) who could make up a story like that?

"Fine," I said. "I'll tell you everything."

Cheese Breath leaned back against the stone fireplace on the far wall, settling in to listen to my story. The other two merely stood there, just feet away, and listened intently while I spoke about that night in the chapel, the text messages, the assignments. By the time I was done, I actually felt a little better. The pressure that had been permeating my chest for the past several days was gone. I'd finally spilled the whole thing.

"And that is the whole true story," I said, lifting my chin as I looked each of them in the eye.

Zit Lady and Gruff glanced at each other. Then, ever so slowly, Zit Lady leaned over me. "That, my friend, is the saddest, most ridiculous load of crap I have ever heard."

And then they started to laugh. A huge sob welled up in my throat, choking off my air supply and bringing a fresh wave of tears to my eyes. Cheese Breath doubled over, as Zit Lady wiped tears of mirth from her face.

"Kids today," Gruff said, shaking his head as he walked by me and out the door.

His two friends started to follow, and my entire body seized up with fear.

"Wait! Where're you going?" I demanded, my words broken and choked.

"We're going to leave you in here for a little while to think about whether or not you want to repeat that little piece of fiction to the FBI," Zit Lady said. "Don't worry, Miss Brennan. We'll be back. Eventually."

Then the door let out a loud creak and slammed shut behind them.

"Wait! You can't just leave me here!" I shouted.

But their laughter was growing softer and softer. I heard the three car doors pop as they got in the car; then I heard the engine rev.

They didn't pull away, however. Probably just sitting out there with the heat blasting, retelling my story and laughing their asses off. I looked around the room for the first time, the moonlight streaming through the window behind me affording the only illumination. The floor was covered in dust and the rest of the windows on this level had been boarded up. I wondered if the cops had locked the door behind them. Then, I looked down at my hands. They had uncuffed me. They had left me alone inside a house with who knew how many doors and windows, completely free to move around.

It was as if they were begging me to run. What the hell kind of cops were they?

I got up from my chair, my heart pounding in every one of my veins. Could I run? Where would I go? Did it even make any sense? I hadn't done anything wrong. Maybe these losers refused to believe me, but the FBI would have to. They had zero evidence against me. None. As much as my flight reflex was urging me to take the opportunity and get the hell out, my logic got the better of it. I had nowhere to go. At least, nowhere they wouldn't find me. My best bet was to stay here, try to keep warm, and wait to see what happened next.

Just as I made this decision, my phone beeped.

I jumped halfway across the room and fumbled it out of my pocket.

ASSIGNMENT NUMBER FIVE: BEHIND THE HOUSE THERE'S A GATE. YOU'LL FIND A NOTE TUCKED THROUGH THE LOCK. THIS NOTE WILL LEAD YOU TO NOELLE.

First my heart sunk into my toes. A fifth assignment? They had said there would be four. But then, just as quickly, my skin started to sizzle. The cops were wrong. Noelle was alive. I could still save her.

And just like that I knew. I knew like I knew my own birthday. Those people were not cops. They were in on this somehow. They had brought me out here, left me in the house alone, so that I could get this text and be sent off on the latest mission.

Adrenaline racing through my veins, I turned around and stepped to the side of the window, peeking around the frame. The cops were still sitting in their car, gabbing away, the overhead light on in the backseat so I could see Zit Lady's laughing face. Did they know I'd already gotten the text? Were they supposed to follow me if I fled? The thought of those three trailing after me in the dark was not one I relished. All I knew for sure was that right then, no one was even looking in my direction. If I wanted to get out of here on my own, it was now or never.

On my way to the back of the house, I grabbed Gruff's hat and gloves. The floorboards seemed to grow louder as I raced down a hallway, through a decrepit old kitchen to the back door. I tried the knob, but it was locked, the windows boarded over. Desperately, I whirled around, looking for another way out. Something moved in the corner of my vision and I flinched, but it was just an old, flimsy curtain, billowing in the breeze. I brought my hand over my heart and took a deep breath.

Wait. The breeze. That meant there was an open window.

I raced out the side door of the kitchen into an old, dusty library.

The window behind the desk on the far side of the room was broken, with no board to cover it. I reached up and used all my strength to turn the lock, which had been painted over about ten thousand times. Finally, it cracked free and I was able to shove open the huge frame, using both hands and all my body weight.

Far preferable to climbing past the broken pane. But I would have done it, if I'd had to.

I stuck my head out and glanced toward the front of the house. I was well out of view of the driveway and the car. I tugged Gruff's gloves on over my frigid fingers, pulled his still-warm hat down over my ears, and climbed out. My snow boots sunk into the six inches of untouched snow outside the window. I took one second to ponder how completely insane this all was, and then I turned and ran.

DETOUR

The white scrap of paper was there as promised. It had been rolled into a tiny scroll. My fingers shook as I extracted it from the lock, knowing someone must be watching me, as they had been all along. I could practically feel them breathing down my neck. I clasped the note in one hand and removed my glove so I could open the note. Tilting it toward the light from my cell phone, I read the words that would hopefully lead me to Noelle.

TAKE THE PATH INTO THE WOODS. DO NOT VEER FROM THE PATH. YOU'LL SOON COME TO AN UNLOCKED SHED, AND THERE YOU WILL FIND FURTHER INSTRUCTIONS.

Further instructions? Why couldn't they just give it all to me now?

Cursing under my breath I shoved the note into my pocket and pulled the glove back on, squinting into the woods behind the gated yard. I knew it must be pitch-black under the cover of the thick trees, but what could I do? I wasn't about to go back to ask the bad guys for a flashlight. Right now, all that mattered was finding Noelle. If she was out there, alone in the woods somewhere, she was probably terrified and about to freeze to death. There was nothing to do but go forward.

I unlatched the gate and pulled it toward me. It let out a squeal roughly the same decibel level as a sonic boom. Behind me, I heard a shout. That was when I started to run. I raced across the small space of snow between the fence and the woods and dove under the low branches crossing over the path, my foot slipping out behind me in the wet snow. My breath already came in ragged gasps, as if I had sprinted a mile in ten seconds. One glance over my shoulder told me no one was gaining on me, no one was on my tail. But then I saw the footprint I had left in the snow and realized it would only be a matter of minutes. In this terrain, they could track me anywhere. Besides, they probably knew where I was headed anyway. My only hope was to get them off my tail. To confuse them long enough that they'd give up—long enough that they'd leave me out here alone to do what I had to do.

Don't veer off the path.

So much for that. This was a matter of survival. Mine and Noelle's. I took an abrupt turn, and dove into the trees. Shoving aside branches and jumping over a fallen log, I tried to keep my bearings. If I could keep a straight line and remain perpendicular to the original path, then I'd be able to find my way back. I had to get to my hands and knees to crawl under the low-hanging bows of an evergreen, and when I stood up again, muddy pine needles clung to the legs of my jeans. At least Gruff's gloves were vinyl and waterproof. Nothing could touch my fingers in those. After what felt like an hour of jogging, jumping, ducking, and the occasional scratch to the face, I glimpsed a huge oak tree looming up into the sky. The perfect hiding spot. I ducked behind it, took a deep breath, and attempted to calm my wildly beating heart. I tried my best to listen.

There was nothing. Wind swirled through the bare branches overhead, but other than that, silence. Had I just imagined that shout? Or had I gotten so far away from the path that I couldn't even hear them coming after me?

I tugged my phone out of my pocket, cupped my fingers around it just in case, and hit the screen to light it up. The time read 9:46. And the battery indicator was seriously low. Perfect. That's what you get for leaving your phone on twenty-four-seven waiting for psycho kidnappers to text. For a split second I thought about calling Josh. Thought about telling him everything and having him call in the cavalry. But the original instructions still applied. Tell anyone and she dies. I was on my own. I shoved aside my frustration and I told myself I would give it five minutes. Wait until 9:51. Then I would start back for the path.

Those five minutes dragged on for days. The longer I stood still, the more alone I felt, the more scared, the more frozen. I had to get moving. I took my first step the moment the clock ticked over.

Okay. All I had to do was retrace my steps. No problem whatsoever. Just keep to a straight line and I'd find myself back on the beaten path. Then all I had to do was hook a right and the path would take me to this shed, which would lead me to Noelle. I turned my phone on to the flashlight app to help guide my way.

I stepped over a thick branch I remembered vaulting over moments ago, then shuffled through a pile of wet, fallen leaves. Soon I was passing through a semi-familiar clearing. But then I paused. That evergreen I had ducked under . . . hadn't it been right on the periphery of this clearing? Dead ahead, all I saw were white birches and elms. Not an evergreen among them.

Instantly, my heart started to panic. I turned around, looking for the evergreen. And there it was, just to my right. I took a deep breath and blew it out. I must have just gotten confused in the dark. No worries. Now I was back on the right track. This time, I walked around the tree, not feeling so daredevilish now that I wasn't being chased, and continued on my way.

It took about five minutes for me to figure out it was the wrong way. Because I hadn't jumped the little stream I was now standing beside. And I was sure I hadn't come down that small hill on the other side.

Okay, Reed. Don't panic. Do not panic. Just go back to the clearing and see if there are any other evergreens. Maybe you picked the wrong one.

But when I turned around again and retraced my steps. I couldn't even find the clearing. It was right there a second ago. Right there. And it wasn't small. How could I have lost an entire clearing in the space of five minutes?

Now my pulse really started to pound. I was lost. Plain and simple.

Noelle was out there somewhere, counting on me, and I'd gotten myself completely lost. All I'd had to do was stay on the path. Stay on the damn path. And I would have found the shed by now. I could have outrun Gruff and Cheese Breath and Zit Lady. And if I had, I could have gotten the next instructions, found Noelle, and the two of us could have hidden in the woods together until the coast was clear.

"So stupid," I whispered to myself, turning in a circle. "So, so stupid!"

Why didn't I ever stop to think? Why did I have to make such rash decisions? This was a life or death situation I was in here. And I just jumped off the path? Who did I think I was anyway, some *Survivor* star?

"Okay, wait," I said to myself, stopping my crazy, dizzying circle. "This is not the end of the world. You survived days alone on an island, you can survive this."

Of course, there was a difference. At least on the island it had been warm. If I spent another hour out here I was going to freeze to death.

Then, suddenly, my phone vibrated in my hand. My heart leapt into my throat. There was one more difference. Here, I had my phone.

The vibration was a text from Portia asking where the hell I was. I yanked off my gloves and started to text back, but then paused. What was I going to say? That I was lost somewhere in Soldier Woods and to please come find me? Telling her that would mean Noelle's death. What the hell was I supposed to do?

I looked down at the half-written text and was about to just finish it. Let her read it and call the cops. Maybe they could get here before the kidnappers figured it all out and hurt Noelle. I couldn't do this alone anymore. I didn't even know where I was. But then, the screen suddenly went blank.

"No," I said, hitting the screen over and over again. "No, no, no!"

Shouting, of course, wasn't going to do anything. The battery had died. And now I really was on my own. I stuffed the useless tech into my back pocket and told myself this was not the end of the world. Just pretty damn close.

My stomach grumbled audibly and I suddenly wished I had eaten more of that biscotti Tiffany had offered me back at the solarium. A stiff wind rattled the trees around me and I flipped up the collar of my coat, cuddling down into its warmth. It was time for me to find some kind of shelter. Someplace at least a little bit out of the elements where I could stop and think. Figure out what I was going to do next.

I kept walking in the general direction of the clearing—or at least where I thought the clearing would be—and came upon a little circle of evergreens. I stooped down to see between their trunks. Inside the circle was a bed of fallen needles, all dead and brown, and they appeared to be dry, as though the crisscrossed netting of branches above had protected them from the snow and rain. Turning to the side, I shimmied my way through the space between two trunks and sat down. I waited for wetness to seep through my jeans, but my butt stayed miraculously dry. It was far warmer inside as well, shielded as I was from the wind. I curled my dirty wet knees up under my chin, held my legs to me, and took a deep breath.

Okay, Reed. Just think, I told myself, listening to the wind above and the rhythmic creak of the branches as they swayed back and forth. *Just think. There has to be a way out of here. There just has to be.*

FOLLOWED

I woke up with a start and cried out in pain. My face was on fire. I yanked it away from the cold bark on which it was resting and winced as my delicate skin tore. Ripping off one glove, I reached up to touch my face. It was all mottled and dented and raw. When I pulled my hand back, there was blood on my fingertips. I had fallen asleep with my face pressed into the trunk of a tree, and now I was bleeding.

I had fallen asleep.

"Sonofa—"

I jumped up and smacked my head into a branch. At least it was a soft, bendy one and not one of the hard thick ones. But still, I momentarily saw stars. Sitting down again to take a breath and get my bearings, I heard something crinkle. There was a stark, white envelope sticking out from under my butt. It practically glowed in the dark.

Where the hell had that come from?

My frigid fingers were barely able to tear the thing open, but I managed to extract the small card inside. Unfortunately, it was still dark out, and as much as I squinted, I couldn't make out the writing.

Letting out a string of curses that would have sent my mom sprinting for a bar of soap to shove in my mouth, I crawled out of my hiding space and into the woods. It was slightly lighter out here. The sun was starting to come up. How the hell long had I slept? Unbelievable. I couldn't seem to pass out in my own bed no matter how hard I tried, but in the middle of the freezing cold woods? No problem. Just call me Reed Van Winkle.

I walked, squinting and feeling my way through the trees and the underbrush, until I came to a slight clearing where the dim light of morning filtered through the trees. I held the card out in front of me, angling it until I could read it.

WALK EAST SEVEN MILES. YOU WILL COME TO AN OBSERVATORY.

THERE YOU WILL FIND YOUR FRIEND.

My heart slammed into my ribcage. Finally. Finally I knew where to find Noelle. But then, just as suddenly, a realization hit me in the gut. Someone had left this note for me. Someone had crept up beside me while I was sleeping. Someone out here was following me. And they had gotten disturbingly close right when I was at my most vulnerable. Was it Officer Gruff? Zit Lady? Cheese Breath? All three of them? Were they all out there right now, watching me, ready to pounce?

Terrified, I turned around and started walking. All I wanted to do was get away from my stalkers as quickly as possible. Show these

people they hadn't gotten to me, that I wasn't freaked. Even though I
so was. Then, suddenly, I paused. There was, of course, just one small
problem.

Which way was east?

I looked up at the wan sunlight. The sun rises in the east and sets
in the west, right? But with all the trees surrounding me, I couldn't
tell for sure which direction the light was coming from. If I had my
phone, I could probably download some compass app, but I didn't
have my phone. My phone was dead.

My phone was dead and my hands were frozen and my nose was
running and my cheek was bleeding and I couldn't feel the middle
toe on either foot, which just could *not* be a good sign. My creaky fingers curled into fists, crumpling the card and the envelope inside my
reddened palms. I'd had just about enough of this crazy-ass game of
scavenger hunt.

"Hey!" I shouted, startling a few birds out of the trees overhead.
A couple of squirrels skittered out from behind a tree and ran up the
trunk, their little claws scraping irritatingly as they went. "Hey, you! I
know you're out there! Somebody left these instructions for me!"

I turned in a slow circle, staring into the dusky, gray forest of trees
around me. Feeling as if I could rush and tackle the first person who
dared step out into view. "Well, guess what, people!? I would just
love to keep you entertained with my wild–goose chase abilities, but
there's the tiny issue of not having a clue which way east is!" I took a
breath, gulping in the cold, dry air. "So if you want to throw me a clue
here, give me some kind of sign? That would be really frickin' great,

because my feet are about to freeze off and in about five minutes I'm going to be no good to you at all!"

I stopped yelling and looked around. Listened for the sound of footsteps, laughter, breathing. But I heard nothing.

"No? You're not gonna help me out here!?" I demanded of the forest. "Because then we're just going to have to wait until the sun rises some more and I can tell which direction it's coming from. Are you prepared to wait that long?"

I closed my eyes and listened. Said a little prayer. Nothing. No response. The frustration mounting inside of me was too much to bear. I leaned forward and let out a guttural scream totally worthy of some big-screen, multimillion-dollar cavewoman production. Like I was summoning my army of mastodons to come trample the enemy.

I wished.

"Fine!" I shouted when I was done. "Fine. I guess we just sit here, then."

I turned around, sat down on the first rock I saw, and obstinately waited for the sun to guide my way.

FLAIR

Hours had passed. Days. Weeks. And I was still walking toward the sun. Shoving aside branches, tripping over stones and fallen limbs, sweating down my back and under my arms, while my cheeks and fingertips and toes froze to numbness. How far had I come? How far was seven miles? I knew I could run a mile on a wide-open track in about seven minutes. How long did it take to walk just one through underbrush and overbrush and mud and muck and ice?

My only ray of hope, the only small change in my fortunes that gave me a smidgen of optimism, was the fact that for the past half hour or so I'd been going uphill. It was murder on my thighs and glutes, and there was a lot more slipping and sliding involved than when I'd been on flat terrain, but at least it was something. Because if there was, in fact, an observatory out here somewhere, it would have to be at the top of a hill. A hill meant I was getting somewhere, that I was getting closer to Noelle.

The hill suddenly grew steeper. So steep that I found myself grabbing on to tree trunks to speed my way, hoisting myself upward with the help of a few sturdy branches. It was nice to use my arm muscles for a little while, give the legs a bit of a break, but soon I started to pant from the exertion. Then, just as suddenly as the incline had begun, it leveled out. I squinted through the trees up ahead. Was that a building in the distance? My heart skipped an excited beat. I'd found it. I'd found her.

That was when I heard the tree branch snap behind me. I whirled around, my eyes scanning the forest. I took a deep breath, waited a moment, and scanned, just to show my stalker I wasn't afraid. Nothing. I turned and started moving again, faster this time. Better safe than sorry.

There. That crunch. That had definitely come from behind me. I upped my pace, glancing over my shoulder again. It had to be pushing noon by now, but the sun didn't seem much stronger. The forest was still all shadowy and the shifting branches played tricks on my mind. For a second, I thought I saw someone lurking behind one of the fatter trees, but on second glance, it was only a huge knot in the trunk, protruding out from the side.

I turned around again, and started to run. At first all I could hear were my own footsteps pounding the ground beneath me, the sound of my own ragged breath. But then, I heard the unmistakable sounds of another runner. Someone else was behind me in the woods—someone who was gaining on me. An owl was frightened from its roost and took off with a series of angry hoots, its massive wings making a racket up above. My heart vaulted into my mouth, but I kept running toward the edge of the woods, just praying I'd get there before whoever was behind me caught up.

I hurtled myself out of the tree line and into the clearing surrounding the observatory, expecting to be tackled or grabbed or smothered at any moment. But when I turned around again, there was no one there. Nothing but trees and snow.

My mind was messing with me. I'd imagined the whole thing.

Maybe.

Taking as deep of a breath as I could, I faced the white dome of the observatory. All around it, the sky was brightening, the morning blue chasing away the grays and pinks and purples of dawn. For a moment, I nearly sagged with relief over having found it, over having escaped the phantom stalker in the woods. But then I remembered: My mission wasn't complete. Noelle was somewhere inside. The last time I'd seen her, she'd been terrified. She'd had a huge gash in her cheek. What if they'd done worse to her since then? What if she was inside this place, beaten and bruised and bleeding and crying?

With one last shot of adrenaline, I raced to the nearest door, a big, blue metal one marked DELIVERIES ONLY. I yanked at it and it opened with a wail. The warmth of the indoors rushed over me. From scalp to toe I felt nothing but relief, and I gave myself a moment to relish it. My eyes took a moment to adjust to the dark. When they finally did, I found myself in a long, stark hallway. I walked along quietly, unsure of which way to go, unsure of who might be waiting for me when I got there. Finally I came to a set of doors. To my left was a storage room; to my right, a lab; straight ahead, the observatory dome, which housed the massive telescope.

Well, these kidnappers certainly had a flair for the dramatic, and I had a feeling the dome would be a more dramatic setting than either of my other two choices. I took a deep breath and pulled open the door in front of me.

A rush of cool air hit me in the face. Beneath my feet, thin, dark blue carpeting covered a shallow, circular staircase leading up. Quietly, carefully, I started up the stairs, holding on to the wooden railing along the wall. The place was deathly still, but I knew that I wasn't alone. And for the first time in all of this, I started to feel real and total fear for my own life.

What was I doing here by myself? What was I going to find when I came around this bend? What if some sadistic serial killer with a fetish for brunette, teenaged soccer players had grabbed Noelle and murdered her and I was next? What did I think I was going to do if I was faced down by the kidnappers? What if I actually had to fight to save Noelle's life, not to mention my own? Nobody knew where I was right then. Not a soul. The kidnappers had made me keep all of this a secret, so that no one would even be suspicious if I didn't show up for breakfast. Except, maybe, for Josh. But thanks to task number four, it wasn't like he was going to be looking for me anyway.

All of these horrifying, unanswerable things flooded my brain as I moved forward, as I continued to climb. But I had come this far. I couldn't turn back now. Even if I could, where would I go? How would I get there? I was injured and starving and exhausted with no phone and no idea where the hell I was. It was move forward, or just stop. And stopping was not an option.

Then, finally, breathlessly, I came to the top of the stairs. Looming high above was the most tremendous telescope I had ever seen, its tip pointing out through the massive hole in the dome ceiling high above. And sitting in a chair directly beneath the scope, her hands tied behind her back, her body drooping forward so that her hair hid her face entirely from view, was Noelle.

SISTERS

"Noelle!" I whisper-shouted, my voice hoarse. She didn't look up. I ran across the cavernous dome and dropped down on my knees in front of her. "Noelle! Are you all right?"

My heart flooded with relief as she lifted her head. She was alive. Thank God!

"Come on! We have to get you out of—"

My words died in my throat. Wait. Noelle looked perfectly fine. She looked gorgeous, in fact. There was no cut on her cheek as there had been in the video I'd been sent. Her dark hair was glossy and freshly blown out. Her makeup had been carefully applied. She wore a dark pink silk top beneath a black cashmere cardigan, and when she removed her hands from behind her back and laid them in her lap, I saw that her fingernails were even manicured.

"Hi, Reed," she said with a smile.

My empty, panicked stomach contracted so fast I thought I might implode. I stood up, my still frozen kneecaps creaking, and took a step back. As I did, I saw movement out of the corner of my eye. There were entry doors all around the circular room, and a dozen women stepped into view, each wearing a flowing black robe, and carrying a dark purple candle. Instantly, memories of Billings House rituals past flitted through my mind. The sisters in black, the neophytes in white. The candles, the circle, the vows. Bile rose up into the back of my throat. I felt so faint, I had to reach out and touch the protective railing around the telescope. It was ice cold beneath my already chilled fingers.

"This was a setup," I heard myself say as my eyes fluttered closed. "You did this." I opened my eyes again and focused on Noelle. On my friend. The girl I had been terrified for—had ruined my life for. The girl who was slowly, gracefully, healthfully rising from her chair. "You did this to me," I said, ignoring the women who had closed into a tight circle around us. They didn't matter. Whatever they were doing there, I couldn't have cared less. This was between me and Noelle. Me and my best friend. Me and the one friend other than Josh whom I trusted more than anyone else on the planet.

Strike that. The friend I *used to* trust more than anyone else on the planet. Noelle had completely screwed with my mind and my heart. Not to mention my boyfriend, my schoolwork, my criminal record, and my entire life. She was responsible for all of it.

"You set me up just like you did sophomore year," I said, feeling exactly like I had in the moment I'd heard that stealing that test for Ariana was a joke, that all the crap I'd found in Kiran and Taylor's room, in Noelle and Ariana's, had been planted there for me. This is the way I felt upon learning that everything my friendships were based on had been a test.

I felt like an idiot all over again. A naive, dupable dunce. Like Noelle and everyone else in the world was laughing at me.

"You don't understand, Reed," Noelle said, taking a step toward me. Her eyes shone with some kind of emotion, though whether it was amusement or pride I couldn't tell. "We had to do this to be sure. We had to know that you could handle it. We needed you to prove you are who we thought you were."

"Oh yeah? And who do you think I am?" I spat.

Noelle smiled. "My sister."

There was a mushy lump of disgust growing exponentially in my throat. I wanted to throw it up on her Gucci boots. Wanted to reach over and tear her hair out. Wanted to somehow make her feel like a giant pile of fetid dog crap—exactly how she was making me feel.

"Your sister? Are you insane?" I shouted. "I am so sick of this shit! This is how you treat people you supposedly love?"

I spotted a red leather bag behind Noelle's chair, which I recognized as one of hers, and stormed past her. Dropping to my knees, I dug through her stuff and yanked out her phone.

"Reed, what're you doing?" she asked.

"I'm getting the hell out of here."

I scrolled through her contacts until I found Sawyer's number, then hit dial. The phone started ringing in my ear as I stood up and walked toward the circle of middle-aged and elderly women who had surrounded me—*sisters*. The two ladies in front of me didn't budge, one older, white-haired, and straight-backed, the other forty-ish, slightly pudgy, and soft-looking. They both stared at me with amused and almost wondrous expressions. So I took one of their candles and threw it on the ground in the center of the circle. Noelle jumped back. The flame hit the carpet mere inches from her feet.

Everyone gasped and the crowd parted, just as Sawyer picked up the phone. I shoved through to the other side, heading for the stairs and the door beyond.

"Hello?" He sounded groggy, like I'd woken him up. "Noelle? Is that you? Is everything okay?"

"It's not Noelle, Sawyer, it's Reed," I said. "I'm so sorry for waking you up."

"Reed?" He was fully awake now. "What's going on? Are you all right?"

"No, not really," I said, gunning for the door. I could hear the commotion behind me as the women attempted to put out the fire. Noelle shouted my name, but I didn't turn around. "I'm at an observatory somewhere in Soldier Woods. Can you Google map it and come get me?"

"Of course." I could hear the sounds of rustling sheets, of him grabbing clothes and getting dressed. "But how did you get—"

"It's a long story. I'll explain all of it when you get here," I said, shoving through the door at the bottom of the steps and into the warm hallway. "I'll find whatever road it's on and start walking down the hill. Just keep an eye out for me."

"Okay. I'll be there as fast as I can," Sawyer said.

"Thanks, Sawyer. You're saving my life," I told him. "Again."

Then I hung up the phone, just as the door opened and slammed behind me.

"Reed! You can't go!" Noelle shouted. "You don't understand what's going on." I turned around, the fury inside of me so fierce that it took all of my strength, my control, my energy, to keep from screaming at the top of my lungs.

"I understand one thing, Noelle," I said, getting right in her face. "Since I've met you, you've done nothing but preach to me about friendship and sisterhood. But you have no idea what either one of those things means."

Then I lifted her phone in front of her and flung it at the cement floor as hard as I possibly could. I shoved through the door at the far end of the hall, out into the bright, cold sunshine, leaving her behind—for good.

DECISIONS, DECISIONS

"I wish you'd tell me what's wrong," my mom said as I held the phone between my ear and my shoulder and attempted to zip up my Croton High School duffel bag.

I'd just taken the longest shower of my life, standing under the warm spray until the feeling came back into every one of my toes and the scrape on my cheek stopped stinging. It had been just long enough to charge my phone to the point where I could make this call—the call asking my parents if they could get me excused from school for a few days so I could come home.

"There's just a lot going on here and I feel like I need to get away to deal with it," I told her. The zipper finally unsnagged and let out a satisfying *zip* to punctuate my point. "I think I need some time alone to figure out . . . I don't know . . . why I'm really here, I guess."

"You're not thinking of quitting school?" my mother said, alarmed.

I sat down on my bed and sighed, closing my eyes. "Not quitting school. Just maybe . . . quitting Easton." It was hard to even get the words out. Quitting was not usually part of my repertoire. I looked down at the maroon and gold duffel bag. "Maybe I should go back to Croton High."

"Reed, honey. Just think about all the opportunities you'd be passing up," my mother said.

"I know, Mom," I said through my teeth. "But just think about all the crazy I'd be passing up too."

There was a long silence on the other end of the line. I could hear her quietly breathing, could practically hear her thinking. "I just don't know—"

"Neither do I," I said as patiently as I could. "That's why I'm coming home just to think about it."

"Reed, there are some things you should probably—"

"Mom, can we please just talk about this when I get there?" I asked, pushing myself up to standing again. "I have to get out of here soon if I'm going to make my flight."

When I'd returned to my room, my bag—the one the supposed cops had taken from me—and my laptop had been waiting for me on my bed. Those three goons, who must have been hired by Noelle to play their little parts in the charade, had brought my stuff back to my room. After letting another crushing wave of anger pass through me, I'd grabbed my wallet, retrieved my ATM card, and booked a one-way ticket to Pittsburgh. Turned out it was a lot cheaper than the round-trip airfare to Paris I'd priced early last week. I hadn't even had to empty out my bank account to buy it.

"Okay, hon. That's probably better anyway. We can talk it all out face-to-face," she said.

Yee-haw. I couldn't wait. Suddenly I found myself hoping the flight was forced to circle the airport a couple dozen times before landing. I could use the extra alone time.

"I'll call the headmaster, and your dad can fax a signed excuse note from his office," she added. "And I'll call your brother and tell him to drive home for dinner tonight."

Scott. It would be so good to see him. It would be good to even get a noogie from him. At least I knew that he was one person who would never betray me, one person who actually knew what it meant to be a good friend.

"Okay. Thanks, Mom. I'll see you guys soon."

We hung up and I took a deep breath, glancing around to make sure I hadn't forgotten anything. My laptop would be coming with me, but right now it was still open on my desk. My Easton Academy e-mail account was open on the screen. I glanced at the clock. To get my mom off the phone I'd kind of exaggerated about how little time I had before I had to leave.

I pulled the chair out gingerly, my body still recovering from its night in the woods, and sat down. A few of the e-mails were easy deletes—rehashings of lunchtime conversations from friends, a lengthy discussion about whether Lorna should date a sophomore. Then I saw a message from Portia and my heart lurched. Tiffany, Rose, and Portia had to be wondering what the hell had happened to me last night. I'd left them in the solarium doing my homework for

me, promising I'd be right back, and then never returned. I quickly
sent a message to the three of them, apologizing and saying a family
emergency had sprung up and I'd be away for a few days. Then I sent
a quick note to Mr. Barber, explaining the same and basically begging for leniency—just in case I did decide to come back here.

Back in my inbox, there was a week-old message from Ivy. Another
surge of guilt constricted my lungs. I couldn't believe I'd thought
she'd kidnapped Noelle. I closed my eyes for a second and rested my
head in my hands as I remembered, in vivid detail, the insane accusations I had spouted at her that night in the bathroom. She probably
hated me, and with good cause.

Taking a deep breath, I opened a new message and started to type.

Dear Ivy,

I'm so sorry about the way I've treated you, especially that
night in the bathroom. I can only say that I was under a ton of
stress, and didn't really know what I was saying. I know it's no
excuse, and I won't blame you if you never want to speak to me
again. I just wanted you to know I'm sorry.

Love,
Reed

I read it over once and, too tired to quibble with myself over gram-
mar or eloquence, hit send.

Five minutes later I was still sitting there, contemplating a ten-minute catnap, but decided I was too wrecked to even get up the energy to drop into bed, when there was a knock on my door.

My head whipped around and I stared at it. Was it Noelle, come to try to explain again? Could it possibly be Ivy? Maybe she'd already received and read the e-mail. I got up slowly, my heart pounding, and opened the door.

It was Josh. Who should have been in poli sci right about then.

"Hey," he said.

"Hey."

I couldn't move. Couldn't breathe. Couldn't think. My fingers gripped the doorknob for dear life, knowing that if I removed them, I'd probably fall right over at his feet.

"Ouch." He winced and reached out to touch my chin with his fingertips, turning my face to the side to see my scratch. "What happened? Are you okay?"

"I'm . . . whatever," I said, my brain all foggy. "What're you doing here?"

"This," he said. And then he kissed me.

That was when my knees actually did buckle. Josh held me up with both arms and kept kissing me, backing me a few steps into the room and kicking the door closed with his foot. My exhaustion forgotten, all I could do was kiss him back. I had thought I was never going to touch his lips again and now that I was, I couldn't imagine stopping.

He was the first to pull away. His lips were completely swollen, his eyes glassy.

"What are you—"

"I thought about it and I realized . . . it made no sense, you breaking up with me," he said, looping his arms around my waist. "I mean,
we'd fought a little about Ivy and yeah, I'd seen you with Sawyer and
talking to that Upton dude, and it was a little annoying, but then I
realized . . . I trust you. And you trust me. So the whole thing made no
sense. And then it hit me."

"The kidnappers," I said, the word like acid on my tongue.

"The kidnappers," he replied with a smile. "They told you to do it,
didn't they? I was assignment number four."

I nodded. It was all I could muster. How was I going to tell him that
there were no kidnappers? That it was all just a game constructed by
Noelle? He already loathed her. If I told him the truth he would go
ballistic. He'd want to kill her.

But then . . . did I even care? Did I want to be friends with her
anymore?

"So, Sawyer told Graham who told Gage who told Trey that he
picked you up in the middle of Soldier Woods this morning," Josh
said. "What happened? Did you find Noelle?" he asked, leaning back
a bit to look into my face. "Is she okay?"

"Yeah," I said. "She is."

"Thank God," Josh said, hugging me tightly.

"Why? You thought she wouldn't be?" I asked. Hindsight being
twenty-twenty and all, it now seemed kind of impossible to me that
I'd ever thought the whole thing was for real.

"Well, this *is* Easton," Josh said with a sad smirk. "So where is she?
What happened?"

I swallowed hard and took a step away from him. "She's . . . with her family," I said, my tongue curling at the vile taste my words brought into my mouth. "They actually found her, in the end. It's kind of a long story."

His brow knit in confusion, but when I stepped into him again and rested my good cheek against his wool coat, he simply wrapped his arms around me and rested his chin on my shoulder.

"I'm glad it all worked out okay," he said.

"Me too."

"So . . . what do we do now?" he asked. "It's already second period."

"I don't care," I said. "Can we just stay here for a while? Exactly like this?"

"Absolutely," Josh said.

Then he adjusted his arms to hold me a little tighter and I sighed contentedly. He was here. He was back. He was mine.

And I didn't want to ever let him go.

OUT OF PLACE

Sun streamed through my windows on Wednesday morning, so bright my eyes stung when I opened them after a long, deep sleep. I groaned and turned my head to face the wall, wondering why I had pulled the blinds up the day before. Right in front of me was the poster of Sydney Crosby, the greatest hockey player currently on the ice, which I'd hung on my dark blue wall during the couple of weeks I'd been home last summer. It still hadn't flattened out completely and the paper shone like it was brand-new, even though it had been up for almost six months.

I guess that's what happens when the blinds are drawn and a room goes unlived in for so very long. I propped myself up on my side and concentrated for a moment, trying to figure out how many days, exactly, I had been home over the past year or so. Last summer I'd spent most of my time on Martha's Vineyard with Natasha Crenshaw and her family, only pit-stopping here quickly before school started.

I'd been home for Thanksgiving, but not at all over Christmas, choosing instead to go to St. Barths with Noelle and her family, and then meeting my parents in New York for a few days before going back to Connecticut.

All told, I'd probably slept in this bed no more than seventeen times in the past year. Sadness filled my chest at the thought. Was it really so bad, being home? What was I running away from? And what the hell had I been running *to* all this time?

There was a light knock on my door and my dad stuck his head in my room. He'd taken the day off to hang out with me, which was just like him. Scott and I always came first.

"Oh, good," he said. "You're up. I made pancakes."

"Then I'm definitely up," I said. I swung my legs over the side of the bed and shoved them into my well-worn plaid slippers, then grabbed a Steelers sweatshirt out of my drawer and yanked it on. No point in trying to look fashionable for breakfast with the fam. Actually, this outfit would probably win best-dressed at Croton High anyway.

I padded into the kitchen, the strong scents of coffee and frying bacon leading my way. Scott was already sitting in his usual chair at the chipped Formica table, sipping coffee from a Hershey Park mug and scrolling through texts on his phone.

"Nice hair," he said, looking up. "They let you walk around that fancy school of yours like that?"

"Nice face," I replied. "The biology department at Penn State offered to study you yet?"

We grinned at each other. It was good to be home.

"OJ, anyone?" my mom asked, emerging from behind the open door of the fridge. I actually did a double take as I sat down at the table. My mom was already showered and dressed, her light brown hair grazing her shoulders in a perfectly chic cut. She was wearing low-rise jeans and a turtleneck and looked relaxed and happy. And beautiful. For so long she had been sick and depressed and self-medicated, some days never even managing to get out of bed, that I was still stunned to see her healthy and awake.

"I'll have some," I said.

"Please," she corrected, rolling her eyes. She poured the juice into my glass, running her free hand over my hair. "It's nice to have my kids home. Even if they are rotten."

"So, Scotty, when do you have to get back?" my dad asked, dropping a plate of steaming pancakes in front of me. He was still wearing his flannel pajama pants and a sweatshirt, milking his day off for all it was worth. Brownish-gray stubble peppered his chin and his dark hair was slightly mussed. "'Cause it's free puck night at the Igloo."

Scott and I exchanged an intrigued look. The Igloo was the fans' nickname for Mellon Arena, where the Penguins played.

"Seriously? You got tickets?" Scott asked, lowering his phone.

"We can buy them there. What do you guys say? Hot dogs, ice cream, maybe a good on-ice fight or two?" my dad said, wagging his eyebrows.

"I'm in," Scott said. "Who needs a college education anyway?"

"Me too," I said with a grin.

"Sweet," my dad said. "If you're good I'll even buy you guys some cotton candy."

I laughed and cut into my pancakes. Sometimes my dad still talked to us like we were kids. But I didn't mind. Especially not today. This was exactly why I'd wanted to come home so badly. Things were just simpler here. Especially since my mom had gotten sober. As I looked around at my family, everyone but Mom in motley states of dress, all of us chowing down off time-worn ceramic plates, with a plastic bottle of syrup in the center of the table and a scorched coffee pot on a macramé place mat, I just wanted to laugh. Noelle and the rest of my friends would have probably been disgusted, or at the very least amused, if they could see me now. But this was home. This was where I belonged.

"Okay, okay. But it's back to school tomorrow with you," my mom said to Scott as she sat down next to him.

"Me? What about her?" he asked, pointing at me with his knife. "She's the delinquent. I'm only missing one class today."

"Shut up and eat your pancakes," my dad said, smacking the back of Scott's head as he sat. "Your sister's going through a rough time."

I smiled my thanks.

"Yeah, yeah. I've been going through a rough time since the day she was born," Scott joked, grinning at me as he chewed.

"Ha-ha," I replied happily.

And then the doorbell rang.

Everyone sort of froze. My mom looked at the clock. "Who's ringing the doorbell at eight thirty on a Wednesday?" she asked.

"Meter reader?" my dad ventured.

"I'll get it," I said, pushing myself back from the table. I walked down the short hall, past the staircase to the front door, and glanced out the skinny window.

Time stopped. The entire world turned inside out.

Noelle Lange was standing on the cement step in front of my house in Croton, Pennsylvania, along with some elegant, aged woman in a fur coat. A black limousine idled behind them at the curb. I narrowed my eyes at Noelle's companion, feeling a thump of recognition somewhere deep in the back of my brain. I knew this woman. But why?

And then, ever so suddenly, it hit me. She'd been in the circle at the observatory. I'd taken a candle right out of her hands and tossed it on the floor.

OVERWHELMING

For a long moment, I thought about not opening the door. Let them stand there in the cold. Let them stand there long enough to figure out they weren't wanted and then get back in their luxury vehicle and leave. Then Noelle reached out to touch the bell again, and I yanked the door open before she could hit the button.

Noelle started. The older woman, however, didn't move a muscle. It was as if nothing could shake her.

"Hey," Noelle said.

I just looked at her. If I'd been wondering whether my anger had abated, I now had my answer. I was still pissed. If anything, I was even more pissed.

"Hello, Reed. I'm Lenora Lange," the elderly woman said. Her white hair was cut into a soft bob that grazed her sharp cheekbones. "Noelle's grandmother."

"Hello," I said suspiciously.

"May we come in?" she asked patiently.

"I don't know," I replied. I really didn't. I still couldn't imagine what the hell they were doing there.

"Reed? Who is it?" My mother came up behind me, all smiles. She was about two steps from me and the door, when she locked eyes with Mrs. Lange and all the color drained out of her face. Noelle looked at her grandmother warily. I looked at my mom. But then, as if nothing odd had happened, my mom closed the distance to the door and smiled.

"Hello, Noelle," she said.

"Hi, Mrs. Brennan," Noelle replied. "May I introduce my grandmother, Lenora Lange?"

"Yes, of course," my mother said. "It's good to . . . see you." She reached out to shake Mrs. Lange's hand. Mrs. Lange hesitated just a moment then took it.

"Charmed," she said.

They both withdrew their hands. I felt apprehension skitter down my back as the four of us stood there in silence, two on the inside, two on the out. There was something going on here, I just had no clue what it was.

"Well, come in," my mother said finally. Her voice was loud and strained, as if someone had pinched her and she was trying to bite back the pain.

Mrs. Lange crossed into our tiny front hall first, followed by Noelle. She gave me this look that was like an apology crossed with curiosity and giddiness. I got the distinct impression that whatever was happening, all three of them knew about it. But how could my mom have a secret with Noelle and her grandmother?

Once again, I was the naive one. In the dark, as usual.

"Come in, come in," my mom said, heading back to the kitchen. "Can I get you anything? Coffee? Breakfast? We have plenty of pancakes."

I almost laughed. Somehow I didn't see Lenora Lange pulling up one of our rickety extra chairs and tucking in for some Aunt Jemima and Log Cabin.

"No, no. We won't be staying long," Mrs. Lange said.

She paused at the threshold to the kitchen, probably realizing that she and her expensive fur wouldn't quite fit inside the small space along with the rest of us. As soon as my dad saw the woman's face, he paled and looked up at my mom warily. But it was as if my mother couldn't meet his eye.

"Hello," he said to Mrs. Lange.

"Mr. Brennan," she replied with a sniff.

Noelle and Scott looked each other up and down.

"'Sup, Noelle?" he asked, slurping some OJ.

"Scott," she replied.

They had met only once before, on our brief stopover in New York after Christmas, and each had kept a respectful distance. It looked like they'd made some kind of silent agreement to keep it that way.

"Mr. and Mrs. Brennan . . . would you mind if Noelle and I had a private chat with your daughter?" Mrs. Lange asked. Her nose wrinkled a bit on the word "daughter." As if it felt funny to say.

"Uh, sure," my father said, looking over at my mom.

"Actually, I think I'd like to be in that conversation," my mother said shakily.

"Suit yourself," Mrs. Lange said.

"I believe I will." My mom stood up straight and set her jaw. "This is, after all, my house." She stepped past Mrs. Lange and her huge fur, leading us all into the living room. "Shall we?"

As soon as we were all inside, my mom yanked the accordion door between the kitchen and the living room closed. Then she stood in front of it with her arms crossed over her chest, like a sentry. Like she was going to keep us all from bolting. Or keep my dad and Scott from getting in.

"Okay, what is going on?" I asked, walking to the far side of the coffee table. "You guys are freaking me out."

My mom looked at Mrs. Lange and said, "If we're going to do this, let's just do it."

I felt like she was speaking in tongues. Why was she talking to Mrs. Lange like that? Like she knew her? Like she was mad at her?

Mrs. Lange looked at Noelle. Noelle cleared her throat. She unbuttoned her black wool coat, took it off, and slowly folded it over the back of my dad's lounge chair. Then she leaned her hands into it, and looked me in the eye.

"Reed, back at the observatory, when I said we were sisters, I meant it," she said.

I rolled my eyes. "Not this again."

"No, I mean . . . I didn't mean Billings sisterhood, blah, blah, blah," she said, shaking her head. "I meant, we're sisters. Like, real sisters."

"Blood relations," Mrs. Lange supplied. "The two of you . . . share the same father. My son."

I couldn't have been more stunned if she'd reached out and picked my nose.

"What?" I blurted. "No. *No.* I know who my father is. You people are cracked. I can't—"

"Reed," my mother said quietly. "It's true."

"What?" I practically screamed, backing away from her. Backing away from all of them. "How is that even possible? You don't even know Noelle's dad. He lives in Manhattan! He's, like, a gazillionaire! Where the hell could you two have possibly met and—" My throat closed over, choking me before I could complete the thought. "You were married to Dad. You were . . ."

I sat down on the couch and bent in half, my arms around my waist, my head between my knees. Dad. Dad was not my dad. My mother was married to my dad who was not my dad when she'd been with Noelle's dad somehow and made me. This was too surreal. Too much for me to process. Way too much for me to believe.

But then, in the whirl of screaming protestations, a few bits of fact came screeching through. Like the fact that I looked nothing like my father. The fact that I looked a lot like Noelle. The fact that Upton said Lenora Lange reminded him of me. The fact that, in St. Barths, Mr. Lange had been insanely protective of me, had given me the same gift he'd given Noelle on Christmas morning. The fact that her mother had avoided me like the plague.

I looked up, tears streaming down my face, and the three of them looked down at me. My mother looked scared. Noelle looked hopeful. Mrs. Lange, sympathetic.

"We know it's overwhelming," she said.

"No," I replied. "You have no idea."

I looked at my mom. "Does Dad know?"

"He does," she replied.

"Does Scott?" I asked.

"No."

My parents had been lying to me my entire life. Lying to both of us.

"So when I went away to Easton last year . . . did you know that Noelle was there? Did you know we were going to meet?" I demanded.

My mother's face rushed with color. "I wasn't aware of much at that time, sweetie," she said. "But later . . . yes. I did, I did realize that the girl you were always talking about . . . that Noelle . . . was Wallace's other daughter."

"How could you never have said anything? How could you not tell me?!" I blurted.

"Reed, you don't understand. I—"

But I didn't want to hear it. I pushed myself off the couch. "I have to go."

"Reed, come on," Noelle said, grabbing my arm as I tried to get past her. "You can't just keep running away." I looked her in the eye and she tilted her head. "I know this sucks on some level, but think about it for a second. We're sisters."

I felt a pang in my heart, but it was quickly extinguished by the deluge of horrifying emotions.

"I don't care," I told her.

Then I turned and ran out into the cold.

MY GIRL

I didn't come back for a long time. I rode my bike to McDonald's, scored a free coffee from Big Ted behind the counter, and then just sat there, not even drinking it, waiting for Target to open. When it finally did, I crossed the street and went inside and spent at least an hour walking up and down the brightly lit aisles over and over, seeing nothing. Considering I was in mismatched sweats and slippers, I caught surprisingly few disturbed looks.

Finally I realized it was well past time to go home. I didn't want to see my mother or Mrs. Lange or Noelle, but I really wanted to see my dad. I needed to see him. I needed to talk to him and find out what he thought of all this. Why he'd stayed with my mom after she'd cheated on him and produced a baby with another man. Why he'd raised me like I was his own. Why he loved me so much. Mostly I just wanted him to hug me and tell me it was all a big joke.

So when I came around the bend onto my street and the limo was gone and my dad was sitting on the front step, I pedaled all the harder. He stood up when I got to the end of the walk. I dropped my bike on the asphalt and ran into his arms. It was the first time I let myself cry. I just pressed my face into his sweatshirt and cried and cried and cried.

"It's okay, Reed. It's all gonna be okay," he said, kissing the top of my head.

I really, really wanted to believe him. Finally, we both sat down on the step and stared across the street at the Romolos' house.

"What happened, Dad?" I said. "I don't understand how this could've happened."

He took a deep breath and blew it out, making a huge steam cloud in the air. Then he looped his arm around me, warming me from head to toe, and I cuddled into his side.

"You know your mom and I were high school sweethearts," he said. "And you know we moved to New York after I graduated college."

"Yeah," I said.

"Well, after about a year of trying to pretend I was made to be a stockbroker, I wanted to move back here," he said. "As it turned out, I didn't want that life. But your mom, she still did. She was working as an assistant at this big financial firm and she liked going to work every day and getting dressed up and all that stuff. After she had Scott, it was three months at home and then right back to work. For two years we argued about where to live and what to do and then one day we just couldn't argue anymore. We separated."

"You guys got separated?" I asked. "I never knew that."

My father lifted his shoulders. "We never really had a reason to tell you guys. Till now."

I swallowed hard and looked down at my slippers. "So then she—"

"She had an affair. With her boss," he said, nodding. "Right after it happened she came back to me, so upset. She told me everything and said she realized she wanted me. She was just hoping I'd take her back after what she'd done."

"What did you say?" I asked.

"I told her I'd take her back no matter what. I'd just been waiting there for her," he said with a small smile. "Your mom's the one, bud. She just is."

I instantly thought of Josh and felt an ache that almost leveled me.

"We decided to move back here and it wasn't until three months later we realized she was pregnant," he said. "We both knew there was no way it . . . no way you could be mine, but I didn't care. I loved you from the second I felt you kick inside her belly."

I laughed and a new wave of tears rolled down my face. My dad turned slightly and hugged me again.

"You're mine, Reed. No matter what," he said. "You're my girl. You know that, right?"

"I know," I said, my words muffled by my tears.

We stayed out there for a while until my breathing returned to normal. Until I could think again. Until I felt like I'd cried every damn tear I'd ever have.

"Mrs. Lange wants to see you in the morning," my father said finally.

"Yeah? Why? Is she gonna give me my inheritance early?" I joked.

"You wish," he said, giving me a squeeze. "Nah. I think she just wants to know you. And who could blame her?"

I smirked. "Yeah. I'm a real catch. It's, like, one o'clock and I'm still in my pj's with snot and tears all over me."

"Good enough for a hockey game," my dad said.

"We're still going?" I asked, brightening.

"Of course we're still going," he said. "You can't promise your brother an Igloo hot dog and then take that away. He'll kill us both on the spot."

"Good point," I said. I looked over my shoulder at the house where I knew my mother was waiting to talk to me. Waiting for some big, emotional encounter. I dreaded it with every fiber of my being. "Can we just hang out here a while longer?"

"We can," my dad said. "But sooner or later you're going to have to go inside. You know that, right?"

"I know," I said, leaning my head on his shoulder. "Just not yet."

ANSWERS

I guess the Croton Comfort Suites hotel wasn't good enough for Lenora Lange, because Thursday morning my mom had to drive me all the way to Pittsburgh and the luxury hotel room the old lady had booked for herself and Noelle. Scratch that. It couldn't be called a hotel room. It was, in fact, a presidential suite on the top floor of a luxury hotel, the square footage of which, my mom couldn't help noting with awe, was larger than the square footage of our entire house.

"Welcome to my world, Mom," I said as we waited for Mrs. Lange in the opulent parlor area, complete with crystal chandelier, brocade couches, and a continental breakfast spread fit for a queen.

My mother gave me a wan smile. Our relationship over the past twenty-four hours had devolved into a kind of polite silence. We'd barely spoken on the two-hour drive to Pittsburgh, other than to comment on the weather and talk about the game last night. Just as we'd pulled up to the valet at the hotel, my mom finally asked me the one question that had probably been on her mind for two days straight. Was I, or was I not, going back to Easton?

I told her I still didn't know.

"Good morning, ladies," Mrs. Lange said, stepping into the room with Noelle on her heels. She wore a chic black dress with a boat neck and straight skirt, a double strand of pearls decorating her collarbones. Noelle was far more casual in slim jeans and a cowl-neck cashmere sweater. They both stood before us, much like they had the day before at my house. Only they were farther away this time, what with all the space.

"I trust your drive was pleasant," Lenora said.

"It was fine, thanks," my mom replied.

"Good," Lenora said. "So, Mrs. Brennan, if you don't mind, we'd like to speak to Reed alone. Just for a few minutes."

My mother's face turned red, but she didn't respond. She simply looked at me.

"It's okay, Mom. I'll be fine," I said.

"Okay, then," she replied. "I'll wait for you down in the lobby."

All was silent as my mom walked out and stepped into the private elevator. Mrs. Lange was staring at me like, well, like I was her long-lost granddaughter. When the doors slid shut and we heard the *ping* that told us my mom was on her way, she finally made a move.

"Have a seat," she said, extending a hand toward the formal-looking sofa behind me. "Would you like something to eat?"

I backed up and sat down. My stomach was grumbling and I would have killed to tear into one of those yummy, buttery-smelling croissants, but I had a feeling that eating during this conversation might present a choking hazard.

"No, thank you," I said.

"All right, then, we'll just get right to it," she said.

I expected her to sit down in one of the wing-backed chairs on the other side of the coffee table and maybe whip out some blue-backed legal documents for me to sign, swearing that I'd never lay claim to any of the Lange fortune. Instead, she sat down next to me on the couch. So close, our knees were touching.

"Reed, I want you to know I am so sorry about everything I put you through over the last several days," she said, reaching out and placing her hand over mine. Her fingers were surprisingly warm, and she had the hands of a much younger woman. Not frail in the slightest.

"Wait a minute, what *you* put me through?" I said, glancing at Noelle. "I thought—"

"None of this was Noelle's idea," Mrs. Lange said, looking at Noelle as well. "Please don't blame her. She was merely doing what was asked of her."

My brain felt unsteady, like it was resting on a plate of Jell-O. "I don't understand. Why?"

"We needed to make sure that you were ready," she replied. "That you were strong enough for what's to come."

"What's to come? What are you talking about?" I said, my eyes flicking from her face to Noelle's. "How long have you guys known about me? That I was your sister?" I said to Noelle.

"I only just found out, Reed, I swear," Noelle said.

"What does 'only just' mean?" I asked. "Like yesterday or last week or—"

"Right after you started up the BLS," Noelle said.

My heart turned inside out. "That was more than a month ago! Funny definition of 'just,'" I spat. This infraction I could blame her for. "How could you not tell me?"

"I didn't know how to!" Noelle replied, throwing up her hands. "I know how much you worship your dad and I didn't want you to think *my* dad was some kind of philandering man whore. He's not—"

Mrs. Lange held up a hand and Noelle stopped talking instantly. The older woman pursed her lips. I guess it wasn't every day she heard her son referred to as a philandering man whore.

"Who knew what when is not important," she said firmly.

Hell if it wasn't. My blood started to boil in my veins.

"What's important is what the two of you do with this information," she added, looking at the both of us. "What's important is what happens next."

"Okay, Grandmother. You've been talking around this for days. What happens next?" Noelle demanded, ducking her chin as she faced off with her grandma. *Our* grandma.

"Noelle, come here, please," Mrs. Lange said, shifting to make some room on her other side.

Noelle rolled her eyes and sighed, but sat down. Mrs. Lange grasped Noelle's hand atop her leg. Suddenly, my chest was filled with this overwhelming and unexpected lightness. Seeing this woman's hands clasping Noelle's and mine in the exact same way made me suddenly feel like Noelle and I were perfectly and totally equal. For the first time ever. And then, another wave of headiness hit me even harder.

Noelle and I were sisters. Sisters. I had an actual sister. Who just happened to be the person who had alternately tortured and protected me during the past two years. Which, actually, kind of made sense. Wasn't that the way sisters treated each other?

"Haven't the two of you ever wondered what makes you so special? What makes Billings so special? Why you were both chosen to become Billings sisters?" Mrs. Lange asked.

"I thought she got in because you were in, and I got in because psycho Ariana Osgood wanted me in," I said acerbically.

She pursed her lips once more. "Ah, Miss Osgood. So much misplaced potential."

My brow knit at her nostalgic tone. Ariana had turned into a cold-blooded murderer. How could anyone talk about her like she was missed?

"I can see why you might think that, Reed," she said, squeezing my hand, "but it's more than that. Everything happens for a reason."

I felt a chill of recognition go down my spine as Mrs. Lange released our hands and stood. Noelle and I looked at each other with a sort of wary excitement. We both felt that something monumental was about to happen. Something huge.

Mrs. Lange walked over to a small, ornately carved wooden box sitting on a table in front of the window. When she opened it, I could see the dark purple velvet lining the inside. She removed an old-fashioned key, long and gold with a delicately scrolled knob, attached to a purple cord.

"Go to the chapel," Mrs. Lange said quietly, her eyes shining as she dangled the key in front of us. It caught the sun streaming through the window, glinting in the light. "You must go tonight and you must go together. Everything depends on this, girls." She stepped forward and placed the key in my hand, then placed Noelle's hand over it, so that it was nestled between both our palms. Then she looked into our eyes and smiled. "Go to the chapel, my sisters. All the answers are there."

SPECIAL

It was a clear, frosty night, the stars out by the thousands overhead as Noelle and I trudged up the hill on the outskirts of campus and ducked into the woods. Neither one of us spoke, the crunching of the snow beneath our feet, the rhythmic bursts of our breath the only sounds around us. I tried not to think about the night I'd so recently spent alone in the woods, scared for her life, scared for my own. Tried not to think about how it was all a joke, a test of some kind. All I wanted to know right now was what lay ahead.

We arrived at the old Billings Chapel, its spire rising up against the stars, and we both paused for a moment to take in its stark, white beauty.

"Do you think it's possible that the old bat is just off her rocker and we're doing all of this for no reason?" Noelle said suddenly.

"You tell me. She's *your* grandmother," I said sarcastically.

"And yours," she replied.

"Right. But you've known her slightly longer."

Noelle smirked. "Come on. Let's get inside."

We shoved open the heavy door of the chapel and it let out its now familiar creak. Moonlight streamed in through the stained-glass windows, casting colorful shadows all over the room. I smiled, noting for the millionth time how the Billings Literary Society had taken the once dirty, abandoned space and made it cozy and welcoming. The floors had been swept clean, there were fresh candles in the many sconces lining the walls, and up on the platform around the pulpit was a collection of colorful silk pillows, plush chenille throws, and even a fur blanket Vienna had left behind after our last meeting.

I walked over to the first sconce and lit the two taper candles with a match. Then I took them both down and handed one to Noelle.

"Have you ever seen any lock this key would fit?" Noelle asked, tugging the key out of her coat pocket and holding it up.

"No. But I haven't been looking for one before now."

I turned around and started along the right side of the chapel. Noelle took the left. I passed through the first arch in the wall, into the storage area with all the old wicker collection baskets, the shelves full of dusty old hymnals. Nothing. Through the next arch was a tall bookshelf, packed from top to bottom with bibles, more hymnals, and a stack of ceramic bowls and cups. Again, nothing. As I stepped out of the archway, Noelle emerged from the one across the chapel. I raised my eyebrows. She shook her head.

I crossed the room to her and together we walked into the old chaplain's office. There were more bookshelves in here, these mostly bare, and a rickety old desk and chair.

"What about the drawers?" I asked.

Noelle placed her candle into an ancient, brass candleholder atop the wooden surface and tried the drawers. The first two slid open with no problem. The third she had to struggle with since it was welded shut from years of moisture and warping, but it finally flew open.

"Nothing but crumbling paper," Noelle said, throwing her hands up and letting them slap down at her sides.

Holding my candle aloft, I carefully moved around the small room. We hadn't cleaned up in here, so there was still a thick layer of dust on every surface. I saw a small box on one of the bookcase shelves and moved in to take a closer look. As I did, something on the floor caught my eye and I froze.

It was a scratch—a deep, arcing scratch in the wooden floor. It extended out perfectly from the edge of the bookcase, out into the room. Suddenly my heart was in my throat.

"Noelle, come here," I whispered.

"What? What did you find?" she asked, lifting her eyes from the book she was perusing.

"I'm not sure. Just come here."

Noelle dropped the book on the desk and walked over. "Okay, but why are you whispering?"

I paused. "I don't know."

I took the candle and walked around the side of the bookcase. "I think maybe this bookcase swings out," I said, nodding at the floor.

Then I walked around the other side and blinked. "Oh my God. Hinges."

Noelle's eyes widened. "No way. A secret passageway?"

I grinned. "Let's find out."

I placed my candle into an empty sconce on the wall and slipped my fingers into the small space between the wall and the bookcase. Noelle did the same, our arms interlacing.

"One, two, three," she said.

We pulled, and the bookcase swung open like a door. Behind it was another door, small and white, with a keyhole just above the doorknob.

My mouth was completely dry. "Try it," I said.

Noelle whipped out the key again and shoved it into the lock. She looked me in the eye and turned. The click was so loud we both jumped. She turned the doorknob and the small, wooden door swung open with an eerie, groaning wail. I'd never seen Noelle look so scared in my life.

"Get the candles," she said, her breath short and shallow.

I did as I was told and handed her one. We held them both out in the doorway. Their flames danced as they illuminated the top of a slim, winding staircase.

"Okay. So maybe the old bat's not entirely off her rocker," Noelle said.

"Unless we're about to walk into a tomb full of dead bodies," I replied.

Noelle narrowed her eyes at me. "Thanks for that image. That's exactly what I needed right now."

Then she took a deep breath and stepped onto the staircase. It creaked beneath her weight, and she pressed her free hand into the wall to steady herself.

"Wait," I said. "Are you sure you want to go down there?"

"All that matters is what lies ahead, right?" she said over her shoulder. "What's the matter, Glass-Licker? Ya scared?"

I rolled my eyes. "Lead the way."

So she did. Slowly, carefully holding on to the wall all the way, we descended the winding staircase into the ice-cold basement of the Billings Chapel. At the base of the stairs, we each held our candles out in front of us, the flames flickering like wild now, since our arms were trembling.

The room was a perfect circle. Tapestries decorated the walls, and a set of chairs stood in a smaller circle, all facing a thick, wooden book stand that was directly at the center of the room. I took a breath and counted. There were exactly eleven chairs.

"Maybe the BLS didn't hold their meetings upstairs in the actual chapel," I said quietly, staring at the bookstand. I could just imagine Elizabeth Williams standing behind it, the Billings Literary Society book open in front of her. "Maybe they held them here."

"This is it?" Noelle asked. "This is what she sent us here to find? A basement and some old chairs?"

"Wait a second." I took a couple of steps into the room, reaching my candle out in front of me. "There's a book on there."

Noelle and I glanced at each other. That same sizzle of anticipation I'd felt back in the presidential suite went through me now. Together we walked forward, sliding a pair of chairs aside to enter the circle. We parted at the bookstand and walked around it, coming together again in front of the open book.

The pages were yellow with age and covered in dust. I reached out one hand and swept it across the pages, clearing an arc of the tiny script. My heart caught as I recognized the handwriting.

"Elizabeth," I breathed. "This is Elizabeth Williams's book."

Noelle reached out and closed it, kicking up a huge cloud of dust. The silt filled my nostrils and mouth and we both coughed, waving our hands in front of our faces as the air cleared. When it did, we stared down at the inscription in the center of the leather cover, the words as clear as day. Whatever I'd been expecting, whatever I had thought Mrs. Lange was talking about when she'd told us we were special, that Billings was special—when she'd asked us if we'd ever wondered why—it had not been this.

The inscription read: THE BOOK OF SPELLS.

CHARMING GIRLS.
FINE BREEDING.
PERFECT MANNERS.
BLACK MAGIC.

THE BILLINGS SCHOOL,
ESTABLISHED 1915,
WHERE THE GIRLS ARE WITCHES.

TURN THE PAGE FOR
A SNEAK PEEK OF

THE
BOOK OF
SPELLS
a private prequel

Even at the tender age of sixteen, Elizabeth Williams was the rare girl who knew her mind. She knew she preferred summer to all other seasons. She knew she couldn't stand the pink and yellow floral wallpaper the decorator had chosen for her room. She knew that she would much rather spend time with her blustery, good-natured father than her ever-critical, humorless mother—though the company of either was difficult to come by. And she knew, without a shadow of a doubt, that going away to The Billings School for Girls was going to be the best thing that ever happened to her.

As she sat in the cushioned seat of her bay window overlooking sun-streaked Beacon Hill, she folded her dog-eared copy of *The Jungle* in her lap, making sure to keep her finger inside to hold her place. She placed her feet up on the pink cushions, new buckled shoes and all, and pressed her temple against the warm glass with a wistful sigh. It was September 1915, and Boston was experiencing an Indian summer, with temperatures scorching the sidewalks and causing the new automobiles to sputter and die along the sides of the roads. Eliza would have given anything to be back at the Cape house, running along the shoreline in her bathing clothes, splashing in the waves, her swim cap forgotten and her dark hair tickling her shoulders. But instead, here she was, buttoned into a stiff, green cotton dress her mother had picked out for her, the wide, white collar scratching her neck. Any minute now, Maurice would bring the coach around and squire her off to the train station, where she and her maid, Renee, would board a train for Easton, Connecticut, and the Billings School. The moment she got to her room in Crenshaw House, she was going to change into her most comfortable linen dress, jam her floppy brown hat over her hair, and set out in search of the library. Because living at a school more than two hours away from home meant that her mother couldn't control her. Couldn't criticize her. Couldn't nitpick every little thing she wore, every book she read, every choice she made. Being away at school meant freedom.

Of course Eliza's mother had other ideas. If her wishes came true, Billings would turn Eliza into a true lady. Eliza would catch herself a worthy husband, and she would return home by Christmas triumphantly engaged, just as her sister, May, had.

After two years at Billings, eighteen-year-old May was now an engaged woman—and engaged to a Thackery, no less. George Thackery III of the Thackery tanning fortune. She'd come home in June, diamond ring and all, and was now officially their mother's favorite—though truly she had been so all along.

Suddenly the thick oak door of Eliza's private bedroom opened and in walked her mother, Rebecca Cornwall Williams. Her blond hair billowed like a cloud around her head and her stylish, ankle-length gray skirt tightened her steps. She wore a matching tassel-trimmed jacket over her dress, even in this ridiculous heat, and had the Williams pearls, as always, clasped around her throat. As she entered, her eyes flicked over Eliza and her casual posture with exasperation. Eliza quickly sat up, smoothed her skirt, straightened her back, and attempted to tuck her book behind her.

"Hello, Mother," she said with the polished politeness that usually won over the elder Williams. "How are you this morning?"

Her mother's discerning blue eyes narrowed as she walked toward her daughter.

"Your sister and I are going to shop for wedding clothes. We've come to say our good-byes," she said formally.

Out in the hallway, May hovered, holding her tan leather gloves and new brimless hat at her waist. May's blond hair was pulled back in a stylish chignon, which complimented her milky skin and round, rosy cheeks. Garnets dangled from her delicate earlobes. She always looked elegant, even for a simple day of shopping.

Eliza's mother leaned down and snatched the book right out from under Eliza's skirt.

"*The Jungle?*" she said, holding the book between her thumb and forefinger. "Elizabeth, you cannot be seen reading this sort of rot at Billings. Modern novels are not proper reading for a young lady. Especially not a Williams."

Eliza's gaze flicked to her sister, who quickly looked away. A few years ago, May would have defended Eliza's literary choices, but not since her engagement. For the millionth time Eliza wondered how May could have changed so much. When she'd gone away to school she'd been adventurous, tomboyish, sometimes even brash. It was as if falling in love had turned her sister into a different person. If winning a diamond ring from a boy meant forgetting who she was, then Eliza was determined to die an old maid.

"Headmistress Almay has turned out some of the finest ladies of society, and I intend for you to be one of them," Eliza's mother continued.

What about what I intend? Eliza thought.

"And you won't be bringing this. I don't want the headmistress thinking she's got a daydreamer on her hands." Her mother turned and tossed Eliza's book into the crate near the door—the one piled with old toys and dresses meant for the hospital bazaar her mother was helping to plan.

Eliza looked down at the floor, her eyes aflame and full of tears. Then her mother did something quite unexpected. She clucked her tongue and ran her hands from Eliza's shoulders down her arms until they were firmly holding her hands. Eliza couldn't remember the last time her mother had touched her.

"Come now. Let me look at you," her mother said.

Eliza raised her chin and looked her mother in the eye. The older woman tilted her head and looked Eliza over. She nudged a stray hair behind Eliza's ear, tucking it deftly into her updo. Then she straightened the starched white collar on her traveling dress.

"This green really does bring out your eyes," she mused. "You are a true beauty, Eliza. Never underestimate yourself."

An unbearable thickness filled Eliza's throat. Part of her wanted to thank her mother for saying something so very kind, while another part of her wanted to shout that her entire life was not going to be built around her beauty—that she hoped to be known for something more. But neither sentiment left her tongue, and silence reigned in the warm, pink room.

"May. The book," her mother said suddenly, snapping her fingers.

Startled, May slipped a book from the hall table where it had been hidden from view, and took a step into the room to hand it to her mother.

"This is for you, Eliza," her mother said, holding the book out. "A going away gift."

Silently, Eliza accepted the gorgeous sandalwood and leather book with both hands, relishing the weight of it. She opened the cover, her eyes falling on the thick parchment pages. They were blank. She looked up at her mother questioningly.

"Today is the beginning of a whole new life, Eliza," her mother said. "You're going to want to remember every moment . . . and I hope you'll remember home when you write in it as well."

Eliza hugged the book to her chest. "Thank you, Mother," she said.

"Now remember, May is one of Billings's most revered graduates," she said, her tone clipped once again. "You have a lot to live up to, Elizabeth. Don't disappoint me."

Then she leaned in and gave Eliza a brief, dry kiss on the forehead.

Eliza rolled her blue eyes as her mother shuffled back down the hall. Then she bent to pluck her book from the trash, but froze when something caught her eye: May still hovering in the hallway.

"May?" Eliza said. Usually her sister trailed her mother like the tail of a comet.

May looked furtively down the hall after their mother, then took a step toward Eliza's open door. There was something about her manner that set the tiny hairs on Eliza's neck on end.

"May, what is it?" Eliza asked, her pulse beginning to race.

"I just wanted to tell you . . . about Billings . . . about Crenshaw House," May whispered, leaning into the doorjamb. "Eliza . . . there's something you need to know."

"What?" Eliza asked, breathless. "What is it?"

"May Williams! I'm waiting!" their mother called from the foot of the stairs.

May started backward. "Oh, I must go."

Eliza grabbed her sister's wrist.

"May, please. I'm your sister. If there's something you need to tell me—"

May covered Eliza's hand with her own and looked up into her eyes. "Just promise me you'll be careful," she said earnestly, her blue eyes shining. "Promise me, Eliza, that you'll be safe."

Eliza blinked. "Of course, May. Of course I'll be safe. What could possibly harm me at a place like Billings?"

The sound of hurried footsteps on the stairs stopped them both.

Renee rushed into view, holding her skirts up, her eyes wide with terror. The sort of terror only Rebecca Williams could inspire in her servants.

"May! Your mother is fit to burst," she said through her teeth. "Mind your manners and get downstairs now."

A tortured noise sounded from the back of May's throat. Then she quickly gave Eliza a kiss on the cheek, squeezing her hands tightly. "I love you, Eliza. Always remember that. No matter what happens."

Then she released Eliza and was gone.

MEET THE ORIGINAL BILLINGS GIRLS IN

THE BOOK OF SPELLS

COMING DECEMBER 2010

Did you love this book?

Want to get access to
the hottest books for free?

Log on to simonandschuster.com/pulseit
to find out how to join,

get access to cool sweepstakes,

and hear about your favorite authors!

Become part of Pulse IT and tell us what you think!